LUNA STATION
Q U A R T E R L Y

Issue 039 | September 2019

Editor-in-Chief

Jennifer Lyn Parsons

Editors

Rocky Breen • Linda Codega • Angelica Fyfe
Caroljean Gavin • Shel Graves • Cathrin Hagey
Sarah McGill • Cait Ryan • Carly Racklin • Shanna Ross
Tamara Lee Rutledge • Gô Shoemake • Margaret Stewart

LUNA STATION PRESS
NEW JERSEY

First Paperback Edition September 2019
ISBN: 978-1-949077-10-0

Luna Station Quarterly publishes short fiction on March 1st, June 1st,
September 1st, and December 1st. For more information and submission
guidelines, please visit our website at lunastationquarterly.com

For Luna Station Press

Creative Director - Tara Quinn Lindsey
Editor-in-Chief & Founder - Jennifer Lyn Parsons

 LUNA STATION PRESS

www.lunastationpress.com

CONTENTS

Editorial

Jennifer Lyn Parsons

Jennifer Lyn Parsons is a writer, programmer, and maker. With influences ranging from Laura Ingalls Wilder to Jim Jarmusch, her tales feature a rare physicality with details that feel hand-carved. When not writing code or prose, she is also the editor-in-chief of the venerable Luna Station Quarterly. She finds joy in video games, comics books, discovering music new and old, and making things out of wool, paper, and wood.

I've spoken often about the power of storytelling. Of course I'm not the first to talk about this and surely won't be the last. Storytelling is part of being human, after all. Every culture tells stories, and many a book has been written, without irony, about the impact of stories. As interesting as those dissections may be on an intellectual level, I've been pondering what that phrase, "the power of storytelling", really means in practical application. What does that power look like when you see it in the real world?

Worry not, dear reader. I don't intend to take the magic away from stories when I speak of practicalities. In fact, I have found quite the opposite occurs and the magic and wonder I feel about stories is increased when their power is set loose on the world. I've been open to story and in turn it has affected me in ways I never anticipated. In fact, I have a perfect example of what I am talking about and it was this situation that inspired me to write about this topic in the first place.

Currently I'm going through a rough patch in my life. The details don't matter so much, but suffice to say that it is causing enough upheaval that am writing this surrounded by boxes and with no knowledge of where I'll be living in the next month. In addition, this change is completely unexpected and much sooner than my planned move this winter. Not exactly the recipe for stability and comfort, to say the least.

In this struggle, I was seeking a way through the challenges I'm facing on a daily basis. I knew it was going to be a long haul, a couple months of deep uncertainty. While I talk often and at length about self care, I was having trouble finding a foothold, a source of comfort and strength to keep me grounded in reality rather than the infinite horrible potentials woven by my over-active imagination.

Unrelated to all of that, yet with a hint of kismet, I had started watching Critical Role. For those of you who have not seen the show, Critical Role "features seven popular voiceover actors diving into epic Dungeons & Dragons adventures". It streams live on Thursday nights and all episodes are archived on YouTube, which is where I've been watching it. The show is currently a phenomenon, not just among the usual nerds, but also with those who've never rolled a twenty-sided dice in their life.

I could have hopped into the second campaign, currently in progress. But when possible, I like to understand a thing as a whole and I was curious to see how this group got where they are. So, I went back and started at the beginning. As I watched, the show evolved. They got better sets and better cameras. The fandom grew, the subscriber count climbing steadily with every episode. They moved from under Geek & Sundry's wing to their own stand-alone company. These are all indicators of success, but that's not why I was watching, of course.

The folks involved have presented themselves as kind, warm, generous people who care deeply about each other and their fandom. That warmth shines through with every dice roll and message to the audience, and yet this was also not the whole of why I was watching, either.

What has kept me going through this rough patch in my life has been the story. No, not just the story. Despite how engaging, well-crafted, and interesting it is in its random, wandering, sometimes chaotic development, it's the characters that are the heart of this tale. Do not dismiss this as "just" Dungeons & Dragons. The characters go through adventures together as you would expect, but they are also a found family, one of my favorite kind of character portrayals. They laugh, cry, fall in love, and would die for each other and the lands and peoples they quickly come to love and protect.

The fact that they do all this, and are portrayed in-character by a group of excellent improvisers, would be enough to keep my mind occupied in those spare moments of down time. Yet this story is doing more than that. In addition to all the fun and much-needed escapism, there is deep wisdom to be found here.

When one character talks to an inexperienced young man who idolizes the group and wishes to run away from home to join them (this being one of many non-player characters handled by the dungeon master, Matt Mercer), the wisdom that is passed along by the player echoes my own fears about where my life is and where it is going. The characters display courage that inspires me to dig deep for my own strength. They speak of fighting through the fear as I must do now myself. They laugh and pull pranks and drink heady wine and it reminds me that I too must take time to appreciate the joy and beauty in the world right now that I cannot afford to miss, else the sadness and fear will overwhelm me.

Call it synchronicity, magic, or just wild chance, but each time I sit down to watch the next episode, through this story I am given messages, receive the words I need to hear, and am buoyed by the power of the story being woven before my eyes. Anyone can read what they wish into a story, of course. To me, that is not a detriment, but a mighty tool. Being able to take something so simple, created with no intention other than to entertain, and pull that which you need from it like the sword from the stone, is nothing short of magic.

I've found healing, wisdom, guidance and strength in watching a self-proclaimed bunch of nerdy voice actors play Dungeons & Dragons. If that's not a compelling example of the power of storytelling, well, I'm not sure what is instead.

Perhaps for you it's in one of the stories in this very issue. I hope you're able to find what you need in these tales. It may not even be the thing you are seeking, but if something is there waiting for you, I hope it brings you what you need. And if you are doing well and are happy and whole and at peace? Then I hope you enjoy the tales within these pages and they brighten your day. We could all use a little of that and, on those bright and shining good days, that's what the power of storytelling looks like, too.

L S Q | 039

Recovery

Kate Sheeran Swed

Kate Sheeran Swed is the author of sci fi and fantasy shenanigans. She loves hot chocolate, plastic dinosaurs, and airplane tickets. She has trekked along the Inca Trail to Macchu Picchu, hiked on the Mýrdalsjökull glacier in Iceland, and climbed the ruins of Masada to watch the sunrise over the Dead Sea. She currently lives in New York's capital region with her husband and son, and two cats who were named after movie dogs (Benji and Beethoven).

Find her at katesheeranswed.com, where you can snag a free short story collection. Kate is also active on Instagram @katesheeranswed.

Recovery cards come laminated, I guess because the Powers That Be keep expecting people to do something responsible with their four-minute re-dos. Nothing says "I'm going to repeat four minutes of my life for the good of humanity" like lamination.

I'm eighty-six years old, and I can tell you right now that ninety-nine-point-nine-nine percent of the idiots on this planet screw it up royally. Case in point: when I was in my twenties, a man actually used his four-minute re-do to get out of a date with me. One minute I'm sitting at a table not enjoying a salad, and the next I'm on the sidewalk with a note in my pocket.

What a waste. And don't talk to me about time paradoxes. I don't know why I remember the weak-ass salad, or how he could have left a note when he'd never met me, or any of that bologna.

At this point in my life, I don't know a damn soul who hasn't relived four minutes of their life.

Except me, of course.

I'm saving mine for the end.

The way my granddaughter Annie's been showing up at the nursing home every day with trashy magazines and contraband chocolate, I figure the end is no longer a distant-future consideration.

They've stuck me with a toothless roommate named Molly, whose dentures make a disgusting pop when she smacks them out of her gums. Trust me when I say that the curtain between our beds does not keep me from hearing her piss in the bed pan.

Among other things.

I keep my four-minute card tucked between my breasts. It's itchy, but I always know it's there. As carefully as I've treated the thing, the corners are still bent, the plastic grimy. They replaced everyone's cards once, when I was in my fifties, after a cult coordinated to zip back in time and elect their leader as head of the country. For three days, we were all required to wear tangerine baseball caps and speak no louder than a whisper.

That was a mess worth seeing. They had to beef up the laws after that.

I hear Molly suck her dentures into her mouth, so I get a second of warning before she slides the curtain over with an annoying metal *shing!*

I miss doors that lock.

"Heya Penny," she says with a sigh, like this is her sitcom and I'm her sidekick sounding board, "I was just thinking about my four minutes."

No one on Earth *isn't* thinking about their four minutes. It's the one topic of conversation they all have in common: regret.

Ironic, right?

"I was thinking," Molly says, licking her lips. She ought to ask the nurse for Chapstick. Or more water. And a tissue, while she's at it. "What if I'd waited? Used my four minutes to get diagnosed sooner? You know?"

"We all gotta die," I tell her, because Molly needs to hear it.

But Molly laughs like I've said something hilarious. "What'd you spend your four on, Pen?"

My name isn't Pen. I'm not a writing utensil.

My typical cover story is that I used it to fix a botched batch of cookies and long story short, that was how I met my husband. It makes people laugh, and it embodies everything they'd once hoped for themselves.

The truth is, four minutes is a pittance. You can't do a goddamn thing in four minutes.

I open my mouth to tell the cooking story.

Instead what I hear myself say is, "I still have mine."

Molly titters. "Fine. Don't tell me."

***

I used to sleep like the dead. It's a good thing we never had a fire, because my husband, Ray, would've had to take drastic measures to save my life. I would not have woken on my own.

I had good dreams back then, too. Dragons and princesses and knights you could convince to discard their chivalry, if you know what I'm saying.

Nowadays, I'm lucky when I can manage a solid doze. Molly's a good girl and takes her meds, as long as she can have them with juice. Me, I hide the pills under my tongue like a cat.

Which is why I'm wide awake when the Well-Dressed Man shows up. I don't know the guy, but he pauses in the doorway anyway, one hand on the frame. I snap my eyes shut because frankly, I don't feel like giving him directions to the vending machine or whatever. Molly's snores snuffle across the room, and I count to sixty before slitting my eyes open to see if he's gone.

Not only is he still here, he's rummaging in the pocket of my out-and-about sweater, which is hanging on the coat rack.

I could "wake up" and scream.

I kind of want to see what develops.

The Well-Dressed Man finishes with my sweater and moves over to the bedside table to flip through my trashy mags. He's wearing gloves that button at the wrist, like a chauffeur.

He drops the magazines, dissatisfied, and scans the area like maybe the TV's got something to hide.

He turns to me. I snap my eyes shut.

The guy's got some nerve, because his next move is to start patting me down, like he used to work for the TSA. I shouldn't be surprised by this development, and yet I leap out of bed—or, OK, I creak out of bed, but still—managing to bump him to the side as I meander to my feet.

My four-minute card topples out from between my breasts and clicks to the floor.

For a second, the Well Dressed Man and I both stare at it. I don't know what he's thinking. I'm wondering if my back still bends enough to let me get it.

The Well-Dressed Man scoops up the card in one swift motion and rushes for the window. He throws it open and launches himself over the sill.

But not before Molly catches him by the belt.

It's a sight, I'll tell you that. Molly's holding the guy by the pants, bent double by his weight, and he's waving his arms and legs like a bug about to be squashed.

Before I can do anything—like pluck my four minutes out of his sticky fingers—the Well-Dressed Man wriggles out of his pants and falls headfirst into the bushes.

We lean out the window in time to see him run across the lawn, boxers puffing in the wind.

"That was unexpected," Molly says.

"He got my four-minute card."

Molly holds up a brown leather wallet. "That's OK, Pen. We'll find him."

***

Escaping through the window isn't an option for Molly and me—my bones would crack like dry sticks—so we sneak through stairwells and hide behind potted ferns like I haven't done since my teenage years.

I've still got the clothes they dropped me off in, so I'm primed for a night on the town, but Molly's a nightgown girl through and through. Her only option was to put on the abandoned pants. They're tight around her hips, so she left the fly undone and shrugged my sweater on top.

Aside from one close encounter with a night orderly, we escape the nursing home without incident.

I expected Molly to be a bundle of nerves once we got outside, to maybe start squealing about police or nurses. But while I'm half inclined to crane my head and stare at the stars, she's got her eyes on the prize.

"What's he want it for, anyway?" she asks as we totter along, just two biddies on a midnight stroll. I can only shrug. I guess there might be a black market out there for four-minute cards. It never occurred to me.

"If it's something noble, will you let him keep it?"

"No," I say. "I've got plans."

Now that we're outside I can see I've got twenty years on Ms. Molly. Maybe more. Whatever she's got has aged her prematurely, but there's still that light in her eyes. She can't be more than sixty.

She wants to ask about my plans. I can see it in the way she's tonguing those cheap-ass dentures. But she keeps her mouth shut, and I like her a little bit more.

We take three buses to get to the neighborhood on the Well-Dressed Man's ID card, followed by a two-block trek and a flight of stairs. If this trip kills me, I'm coming back to haunt the sorry bastard.

There's music blaring out of his door, some kind of candy-sweet pop that makes me want to vomit. His neighbors agree with me, because one of them's banging on the wall and yelling creative expletives I wish I had time to record for future use.

I raise a hand to knock, but Molly must've taken Snooping 101 because she stops me with one hand while simultaneously running her fingers along the top of the door frame.

"There's no way—" I start to say, but Molly removes her hand with a squeak of glee and holds up a dusty brass key.

"You've got to be shitting me," I say.

Molly inserts the key, and we step inside the apartment.

The place smells like a zoo. It smells so much like a zoo, in fact, that I'm amazed the odor of urine-soaked mulch hasn't crawled into the hallway. I grope for the light switch, expecting to see a hundred cats.

It's worse.

The studio apartment is packed with cages that come alive with motion and indignant bird squawks the moment the light flips on. There must be fifty cages in here, lining the walls in stacks of threes. The birds are not your run-of-the-mill pollies wanting crackers. They're exotic as hell, a blinding rainbow of plumage. One of them, near the window, is the size of my torso.

Poor birdie must be dying for a stretch. I can relate.

There are snakes, too, their cages forming a calmer pyramid at the center of the room. If the birds are legal—which I doubt—the snakes can't possibly be. One of them's fat as my arm. And my arms ain't thin.

In a surprising break from the rest of the Well-Dressed Man's decorating scheme, a goat pokes its head out of the kitchen to join the squawking with an irritated bleat.

I hope he's not destined to be a snack for that snake.

Molly claps her hands over her ears, and I turn the light off before the neighbors come bust us for home invasion. It takes a few seconds, but the birds simmer back into their beauty rest. I guess I see why the guy blares pop music when he's not around.

"All righty then," Molly says. "I guess we know what he wants."

I don't see how. "Did the goat tell you?"

"No, silly. The cork board."

"Cork what?"

Molly giggles—I can hardly breathe in this stench, and she's giggling—and fishes a cell phone out of her pocket. She beams the flashlight at the wall.

I think I can be forgiven for not noticing the board through all the feathers and scales. If she wasn't doomed by whatever she's sick with, I'd say Molly should chance a late-life career as a detective.

There's a bulletin board wedged between two bird cages, and it's all gussied up to look like a cage, too. This guy's apparently into scrapbooking, in addition to stealing exotic animals. Makes things easier for us, because he's pasted a picture of a bird at the center of the board: a rare cerulean fluffy-tailed parrot.

OK, I don't know the name of the animal. Or whether it's rare. But it's blue, it's got a fluffy tail, and it looks like a parrot.

It's clearly the Well-Dressed Man's current obsession.

"He's going to use the four-minute card to steal that bird," Molly says.

"If he hasn't already."

"It'd be here."

"True."

She scratches her chin. I wonder if she's got kids or anything. "It's probably at the zoo," she says.

"Probably."

We stare at the creepy paper birdcage and its soon-to-be-sad blue occupant. "Even if we go to the zoo," I say, "it won't help anything. He won't be there. He'll be traveling back in time to steal the bird."

Even optimistic Molly's got no response for that. I sit down on the cage behind me before remembering what's inside. Since I don't want to die via venomous bite to the ass, I slide to the floor instead.

It's probably covered in piss, and I may never be able to get up again, but who cares? My recovery card is gone. There's nothing left to look forward to.

To my surprise, Molly joins me. "What was your plan?" she asks. "For the card?"

I plop my hands in my lap. Pins and needles are already running wild in my crossed feet. "Right before I take my last breath, I'll go back to the moment they dropped me in the home, and I'll tell them not to bother visiting because I hate them."

Molly frowns. She's probably thinking about how she's only seen the one girl hanging around my side of the bed, and she'd be right. Annie's OK, I guess, but surely she'd rather be elsewhere. At least if I go back and tell them not to come, their absence will be on my terms.

Yeah, I know. I'll give you a second to stop weeping over my pathetic old-lady story.

"Why not stop them from putting you in a home at all?" Molly asks.

"You think I didn't try back then? I'd rather tell them to go to hell."

"And you've been planning this your whole life?"

I twist my lips, because really, this kind of sharing is not my thing. But who else am I gonna tell? We're two dying ladies. If she's not exactly old, well, we're still on the same page of life. "I was gonna use it to make sure Ray knew how much I loved him. That was my husband."

I don't have to tell her how the plan went south. She's smart enough to guess it. But now that I'm talking, I figure I might as well finish the story. "The bastard screwed me over and died first. I couldn't even save him with my four minutes, because he made me promise not to."

Molly runs a finger along the cage to her right—bird, not snake—and I can't help but notice how her hand's trembling. She's spending a lot of energy to help me out tonight.

"I used my four minutes to win a hand of poker," she says. "We weren't even playing for money."

Obviously not, since it's illegal to use recovery cards for real gambling.

I can't help it. I burst out laughing. "What were you playing for?"

"Peanuts."

The pun strikes me so hard that I can't keep the giggle from bursting out of my chest. I'm not a giggler—I've never been a giggler—and yet out it pops, rising like a bubble, completely irrepressible.

And then we're both laughing, my stomach aching like I'm trying for a sit-up. My chest squeezes, but it's the good kind of pain, and I don't try to stop it. Molly falls back, literally rolling on the floor. "I gave up my card for peanuts!" she shrieks. It's such a stupid joke, but it clicks the giggle fit up another notch, sending tears gushing down my cheeks. It's such a deep laugh that sobs start hitching into the mix, too, which only makes me laugh harder.

I'm still hiccuping when Molly sits up, suddenly. "I know where he is," she says. "I know why he hasn't used the card yet."

I stare at her, still half drunk on laughter. Or lack of oxygen. "What? Where?"

Molly points to the carefully arranged cork board. "A new bird needs a new cage."

***

The closest pet store opens at nine. The sky's still dark, but we're pretty sure the Well-Dressed Man (a nickname that no longer fits now that I've seen his apartment) doesn't care much about adhering to store hours.

Luckily, it's close enough to walk.

It's hard to believe the guy wouldn't have dashed through the aisles to swipe what he needed as fast as possible before hightailing it to his apartment. But there's a reason he hasn't used the card yet; when Molly and I slip into the store, we find him in front of the parakeet cage, transfixed. He's not as well dressed now, but at least he took a few minutes to pull a pair of jeans over his boxers.

All those fancy birds at home, and he's staring at a bunch of budgies.

Not just staring. Cooing. They hop from perch to perch, oblivious, while the guy who stole my recovery card whispers to them like they're his best buds.

"You take this end of the aisle," Molly says. "I'll sneak around the other side. Then we'll have him surrounded."

"Until he knocks me over with a budgie feather."

I'm eighty-six after all, and I've been up all night riding buses and breaking into weirdo apartments. I'm not exactly primed for a fight scene.

"Got a better plan?"

"Shoot him."

Molly rolls her eyes. I have provoked a sliver of annoyance. Finally. I didn't think the woman had it in her. "All right," I say, "but what am I supposed to do? Ask him nicely for the card back, pretty please?"

"Distract him," she says. "I'll handle the rest."

I'm not convinced, but I don't have a better plan—or any plan—so I follow hers.

When we've sneaked up close enough to hit him with a dog toy, I say, "Hey, you! Burglar!"

The Well-Dressed Man startles. He's been so focused on the parakeets that he genuinely didn't see us enter, even though let's be honest, we're not exactly stealth material. For a moment, he just glares at me like I've interrupted a sacred moment.

"Finders keepers," he says.

Molly's bending to pick up a container of birdseed. She unscrews the top, slowly, and begins to peel the tinfoil lining.

Her plan is something weird, then. Great.

"Creative comeback," I say to cover Molly's rustling. "Stealing a recovery card from an old woman. You should be ashamed."

He shrugs. "What do you need it for? You're half dead."

"You're not wrong," I tell him. "But I don't like it when people take my things."

The man pulls the card out of his pocket like a taunt. "Too late."

Molly balances the birdseed in one hand and shimmies toward the parakeet cage like the world's weirdest waitress. All of a sudden, I understand her plan.

"I'm going to call the cops, young man," I say, taking a step back.

The man moves toward me, teeth bared.

It's all the space Molly needs. She slides the cage door open, simultaneously dumping the birdseed on the Well Dressed Man's head.

The parakeets pour out of the cage and descend upon the smorgasbord that is his head.

You'd think the dude would be thrilled, but apparently feathers in your ears and beaks in your hair are not fun even for the bird-obsessed, because he screams and drops to his knees. I can barely see him through the cloud of feasting parakeets.

Molly slides forward with the grace of a geriatric Olympic gymnast. She flits around the celebrating birds, plucks the recovery card out of the man's hand, and shoves it into mine.

We pull the fire alarm on our way out.

"I hope they catch all the budgies," Molly says as we hurry to the corner to call a cab.

If we lived in Canada or some shit, I'd worry. But it's warm here year round.

I'm rooting for the birds to go free.

***

The first person I see when we stroll into the lobby is my granddaughter, Annie. Her face is ghostly pale, and there are tear tracks running down her cheeks.

When she sees me, she runs.

"Grandma," she says, "what the actual fuck?"

I didn't think I had any more laughter left, but that gets me. It really does. I exchange a glance with Molly, and then we're both giggling up a storm while Annie looks back and forth between us like we've been extremely naughty children. I don't care much about the anger part, but the worry in her eyes sobers me up.

Maybe the girl does care.

"I'm sorry, doll," I say, patting her cheek. Old ladies get to do that. It's practically required. "I needed one last adventure."

Annie hooks her arm through mine, waving off the nurses who look ready to swarm. "Next time, call me. I'll take you on an adventure."

"No bingo," I say.

"You'd prefer zip lining? Rock climbing?"

I pinch her arm. "How about the zoo?"

"You got it."

Annie settles me into bed herself, with a kiss and a promise to return in the morning. The nurses fuss and scold, but I'm perfectly fine. I crab my way through their exams, while Molly accepts the poking and prodding without complaint.

My eyelids are heavy, ready to send me into a deep sleep for the first time in ages, but I switch on my bedside lamp and pull the curtain to look at Molly. Her eyes are closed, but her lips are quirked up like a question.

"You asleep?" I ask.

"Not anymore."

"I'd give you lessons in sounding annoyed," I say, "but I'm not gonna be seeing you much longer."

Molly opens her eyes. "You've got longer than you think. Look at the adventure we just had. You'll probably outlast—"

I untuck the recovery card from my pocket and flick it onto her bed. "I'm not the one who's leaving."

Molly fumbles the catch. The card falls onto her blanket. She just stares, like she's afraid to touch it.

"Go on," I say, "get that early diagnosis. Make 'em cure you. Trust me, you need twenty more years to learn some decent sassing."

"What about telling your family to go to hell?"

I shrug. "I can tell them that any day."

***

I wake from a dream involving a castle and a goddamn *prince*. I'm moving up in the dream world. There's sunlight streaming in through the blinds, a bouquet of flowers in the window.

The other bed is empty.

The chair is not. Annie's dozing with her head propped in her hands. When I say, "Where's Molly?" she startles awake.

"Who?" she says.

"My roommate. You know. Dentures. Incurable optimism."

Annie laughs and rubs her eyes. "I don't know anyone whose optimism couldn't be cured by you, Grandma. But I got you got a private room, remember? The bed's for when I stay over." She yawns, stretches. "I guess I fell asleep in the chair."

I can't help it. I'm grinning. Good for Molly.

It's like I said before—I don't know how it's possible for me to spend my four minutes to give Molly a second chance, and yet still remember Molly to give her the second chance. Paradox, shmaradox. I don't know how this shit works.

Molly ain't here, so I gotta assume she made it.

"Let's get dressed," Annie says. "Still feel like hitting up the zoo?"

I glance out the window again, just in time to see a parakeet land on the sill. He fluffs out his green chest feathers, chirping a pretty song as the sun beams bright and warm.

"Absolutely," I tell my granddaughter, even though my muscles are sore from last night's exertions. "It looks like a beautiful day for an adventure."

The Wiser Move, the Better Choice

Katherine Kendig

Katherine Kendig lives in Champaign, Illinois, where she spends a lot of time reading and a lesser amount of time revising her novel on her extremely slow laptop. Her work has appeared in The Cincinnati Review, Shimmer, Enchanted Magazine, and PodCastle.

Until she was fifteen years old, Rien thought she had free will.

She was Prophecy-touched, which meant the invisible, inviolate Universe cared enough to watch over her, to offer its thoughts and its guidance, as it did for few others. She made her own choices, her own way. But even though she didn't always like it, she always recognized—eventually—the wisdom her Prophecies contained. They offered sensible suggestions. There was no shame in following good advice.

It was a Prophecy that led Rien to Tia. *You will live one year by the sea,* the Prophecy had told her. Rien had been happy to live with her aunt by the sea, happy to stand every day with waves worshipping her ankles and bright fresh breezes whipping her hair across her eyes. She would have stayed forever, if she could. But the Prophecy said one year.

And after all, wasn't there such a thing as being too content? Letting happiness settle too snugly in your soul, making you soft?

So she'd gone away again, back to the plains where only scratching grasses and bloodsucking bugs touched her ankles, where her hair stuck to her skin with sweat. But she'd dawdled too long leaving. There was a new Governor, young and spirited, and he refused to accept the fires that swept the plains every year as inevitable. He'd settled the train engines, with their roaring furnaces and dangerous sparks, in their stations for the summer where they could do no damage. Instead of a fast train, Rien had to wait weeks to join a slow caravan of unhinged boxcars, horse-pulled, dull and safe.

When the caravan came, she met Tia.

The Governor had given women free leave to travel when and where they pleased, but some families were still wary of letting their girls roam. Rien's mother only let her do what she pleased because she was Prophecy-touched. Rien didn't know where Tia was traveling or why, but she had been happy to think that the weeks wouldn't be so lonely. And Tia had been friendly at first—cautiously friendly, until Rien explained why she had left the coast.

Was it wrong, that she was proud to be Prophecy-touched? That her pride crept out in her voice when she spoke of it, even when she complained?

Tia had looked at her the way Rien looked at ticks. Unfortunate, unpleasant, too ordinary for real disgust. She'd said nothing, and Rien had turned and walked away.

Aside from Rien and Tia, there were two old men in the car, who spent most of their time playing cards and wishing they could smoke, and one young man, who spent inordinate amounts of time asleep but when awake would leap from the car and run alongside the track for miles. On the first day, when Tia turned up her nose, Rien had played cards with the old men. Rien didn't know how they could even see the cards where they sat in the shadowy corner of the boxcar; she had to squint and turn her hand this way and that to catch what light she could. She might have spent the whole trip carelessly tossing each carefully chosen card onto the boxcar's dusty floor, but while coins flowed back and forth from one man to another like the tides, Rien's own tide seemed only to go out. So she retreated to her bedroll near the open doorway, where the occasional whiff of air teased her, and she could at least see the sky.

But there in her line of vision, always, was Tia. When the first reach of dawn came into the car and the horses started moving, Tia was there in the doorway, and when the sun set, it turned her the tips of her curls to fire. For an hour every day, Tia jumped off the boxcar and walked beside it. After a suitable delay to demonstrate her wounded pride, Rien joined her. And soon they sat side by side on the hard floor, watching the world pass—first in hills and forest, then in lumpy tangled brush, and finally, lastingly, in flat brown grasses. Light brown, golden brown—even when the plains were green they looked brown through the haze of heat and sun.

Tia had long legs, and she let them dangle out of the open side of the boxcar as they rode. Rien kept hers tucked up inside the car. She didn't want to lose a shoe, she told herself, but really there was something dizzying to her about watching the world move, even slowly, beneath her feet, too far to touch. Tia kicked her legs out, one then the other, and it made Rien lightheaded to watch. But she never retreated further into the boxcar.

They talked about small things. Animals glimpsed in the distance, the occasional flash of flowers that hadn't yet withered in the heat, the irritations of summer and winter and autumn and spring. But eventually, Rien had to ask.

"Are you jealous? That I'm Prophecy-touched?"

Perhaps that was not the best way to ask. Tia laughed, loud and harsh. The old men looked up from their game. The young man was off somewhere, running in the heat.

Rien thought Tia wouldn't answer. Her eyes were on the rocks passing under her dangling feet. Her legs were deep brown, her knees narrow.

"Why would I be jealous of a slave?" Tia said softly. Not softly—quietly. Her voice was not soft at all.

"A slave?" Rien was truly incredulous. She thought that perhaps Tia didn't know what it was to be Prophecy-touched. "A slave to what, or whom? That's a ridiculous thing to say."

"A toy, then," Tia amended.

"I'm not a toy," Rien said, stung by the indifference in Tia's insults. Her arms were locked around her legs, a foot back from the boxcar's edge. Tia lifted her arms and stretched lazily, her legs stiffening straight out, and even in her anger Rien wanted to grab her so she wouldn't fall. She wasn't sure why. It wouldn't even hurt Tia so much to fall—she might bloody her narrow knees, bang an elbow, skin her palms. Maybe she deserved to fall.

Even so Rien tensed, leaned forward just a little. She didn't relax until Tia had contracted, her legs drooping, her hands resting lightly, loosely on the boxcar's hard edge. She wasn't holding on, Rien saw. That was just where her hands happened to lie.

"You're a toy in Prophecy's hands," Tia said, warming to the subject. "You're a fool if you think otherwise."

"I make my own choices," Rien said. She shrugged as if she didn't care what Tia thought, but Tia wasn't even looking at her.

Tia studied one of her own hands, smiling a pointed little

smile. "It's just chance, that your choices always align with the Prophecies?"

"Who says they do?" Rien shot back, but it was the wrong attack.

Tia finally looked her straight in the eyes and held her gaze, and when she asked, "Don't they?" it was beyond Rien to lie. She swallowed. Her face was hot enough to set the prairie afire if she even looked at it.

"And if your mother gave you good advice and you took it," she said, trying to be caustic. "You'd be a toy? A slave?"

"Shocked," Tia said drily, "is what I'd be. My mother gives famously bad advice. She's . . . like you."

"Maybe that's it, then," Rien said. "Maybe you just wish you were important, too."

"Being shackled to the Universe doesn't mean you're important," Tia said. "It just means you're shackled."

"I'm not shackled," Rien said. "I'm noticed. If I become important, it'll be because the Universe paid attention."

Tia shrugged. "The Governor is important. He's changing everything, all over. But he doesn't have any Prophecies telling him what to do."

Rien had no answer to that; the Governor clearly was important, and it was true—he was always going places, stopping just long enough to set some brilliant scheme in motion.

"I feel sorry for you," Rien said.

Tia shook her head. "I'd feel sorry for you," she said, "if I thought you'd understand why."

They had already walked that day, but Tia leapt lightly off the boxcar anyway, stumbling slightly as she landed. She stood unmoving, waiting for the boxcar to pass her, and Rien didn't move either, caught between hoping Tia would never come back and wanting to follow her and explain why she was wrong. After a few minutes, though, she stood and stepped to the edge and cautiously leaned out, holding tight to the door. Tia was four or five cars back, walking next to one of the horses, stroking its neck. She saw Rien looking and turned her head away.

Rien did the same and was startled to see the young man from their car sitting in the dusty grass, sweat-covered.

"It's getting too hot to run," he said by way of a greeting as he climbed wearily back into the car. Rien didn't respond.

***

That night Prophecy whispered in her ear. *Tomorrow when you leave the caravan,* it said, its voice like the last echo before silence, *you will be able to give someone the help they need.*

She thought she heard Tia shifting in her bedroll, maybe sitting up. Other people could hear her Prophecies; usually this made Rien proud. Tonight she wished Tia slept more deeply.

Tomorrow when you leave. Part of Rien, a large part, wanted to stay, just to prove Tia wrong. How easy it would be to show her how awful she was.

But if she left, she'd be able to help someone. Could she deny someone her aid just to make a point to a girl she barely knew? It made no sense. She didn't have to prove herself to a stranger.

She packed her things early the next morning, before the caravan rumbled into motion. She brought as much of her remaining portion of food as she could carry, as much water, her bedroll and spare clothes and bandages. She didn't know where she was going or what kind of aid she would need to give. And there was no reason not to explore for a while, and take advantage of her solitude. She had nothing to do, nowhere else to be.

Tia, of course, was awake when she left; the girl never slept, it seemed. Rien lowered herself carefully off the side of the car and hefted her bag. She meant to simply leave, but Tia was looking at her knowingly, some combination of vindication and pity on her face.

"I'm not going to refuse to help someone," Rien said stiffly.

Tia cocked her head. "If you ever refuse anything a Prophecy suggests," she said, "let me know."

Rien flushed. Again, she wanted to stay; but that was pride, pride and foolishness. Generosity pointed her toward leaving.

"I will," she said. She hesitated. "Don't fall," she added, gesturing at Tia's precarious position. Tia raised an eyebrow.

"I won't," she said. And Rien left, walking along the still and sleeping cars until she came ahead of them, and then striking past on her own.

She let her footsteps steer where they would, curving away from the tracks, curving back in when the grass got so thick and sharp it was like wading through needles.

Midday, she found the young man from their boxcar, collapsed in the grass, ants crawling all over him. She rushed over, looking for injury, slinging her sweaty pack into the grass. But he was only overheated and underwatered, wilted in the sun. Cool water on his face revived him. Rien gave him bread, helped him sit up.

He looked at her, blinking. "Thank you," he said.

"You said it's getting too hot to run," Rien reminded him, irritated.

"It is," he said, unbothered. When they stood, he headed back in the direction the caravan would come from, walking slowly. When he realized she wasn't following, he looked back in surprise; but Rien shook her head, and he shrugged and kept on.

Rien felt bile in the back of her throat. The tracks were only a few yards away; the caravan would be by in an hour. The idiot would have been fine without her. Someone else would have seen him, given him water and bread. There had been no need for her to leave.

She sat down where she was, dizzy, and decided to eat lunch. When she'd eaten, she knew she should get up and keep going, but she didn't. She lay down in the prickling grass and tried not to mind the flies that buzzed around her.

If you reach Harsted within the week, there will be another caravan to take you to the Hygh River.

Another Prophecy—so soon. For a moment, Rien felt a flush of anger. Why Harsted? What was Harsted to her? It was southwest, almost back the way she'd come; if she'd had plans to go to Harsted, she would have left the caravan a week ago.

But it didn't matter what the Prophecy said. It was a suggestion, and this time she wouldn't take it. She didn't want to go to Harsted right now. The Hygh River could wait.

Eventually the caravan would catch up to her. She would simply climb back into her boxcar, and sit next to Tia as if nothing had happened. She didn't even need to tell Tia she was wrong; it was enough to know that she, Rien, was right.

The sun beat down on her head as Rien watched first one car and then another roll smoothly along the tracks behind the tired, sweat-streaked horses. Her own car approached. She saw Tia see her, and took a step closer.

Then a vision hit her: The Hygh River, cool and sweet. She could submerge her heated skin and emerge reborn. The river breeze would dry her skin and lift her spirits. Three weeks at most to get there, if she left now. Months, if she didn't.

"Back so soon?" Tia called. She sounded almost happy. Her long legs swung back and forth.

Yes, Rien thought. But she stood still, half-paralyzed. Her head started to pound. It must be the heat. The damned heat. She couldn't think.

The car caught up to her and passed.

"No?" Tia asked, legs stilling. Rien saw her grip the edge of the boxcar and then let it go. "Where are you going, then?" she asked.

Rien met her eyes. "Harsted," she said, her voice hoarse. The river will be cool and sweet, she thought, pushing the thought down like a lid over everything else. The river will be cool and sweet. She knew it was true, and not the truth.

Tia held her gaze, frowning, as the car pulled away. Rien stared back at her hard, straining her eyes as if she were painting a mental picture, as if Rien's memory of Tia would fade if the painting weren't done by the time Rien looked away. Dark curls round Tia's head like a halo, dark skin faintly sheened in the sun. Rien wanted to kiss one of Tia's stupid knobby knees. She wanted to run up and steal one of Tia's shoes, so Tia would have to come after her. She wanted Tia to jump down and drag her back to the boxcar, and hold her so she couldn't escape to Harsted or anywhere else.

She wanted none of that. She turned away before the heat could bend her thoughts in any more ridiculous directions. She needed to clear her head in cold water. She couldn't wait to reach the Hygh.

"Good luck, Rien," Tia called from behind her. For the first time, her voice was soft.

***

"If you ever refuse anything a Prophecy suggests, let me know."

Rien lived with the taste of the words in her mouth, always. Oh, how she wanted to spit them back at Tia. Let her taste their bitterness.

She had gone to Harsted, telling herself all the while that she wouldn't follow the next Prophecy; the game was up. She caught the promised caravan and took it to the Hygh River; and oh, the river was sweet and it was cold. The Governor had just opened a new iron bridge and flower petals from the celebration still drenched the shoreline; they smelled of spring, of promise, of life.

But then the next Prophecy came, all too soon, and she didn't fight it. Hadn't the flower petals made her crave the rich creamy peaches just ripening in Deston? Why not go there, why not pluck them from the trees herself? What did she have to keep her on the shores of the Hygh River?

Nothing. She had nothing to do and nowhere else to be. And when she left Deston – nothing again. She convinced herself that the Prophecies made sense, that she was making the wiser move, the better choice. She could see the wrongness of her own logic, the way it pushed forward at awkward angles, but still she left, and left again.

She was traveling now for the third time in a year. She had spent the last three years on the move, pushing forward from place to place. In the autumn she took boats down the little rivers as they swelled with rain; in the winter she took trains. In the summer, caravans. She was eighteen years old, now, old enough by the Governor's law to own property, to start a business, to marry. But where would she buy a home or start a business, knowing that every second Prophecy was another leaving? Whom would she marry, when she knew no one?

Rien wiped at the sweat on the back of her neck. She hated the heat, but she sometimes felt like sweat was all that kept her from drying out hollow and blowing away. She sat at the edge of the boxcar in the dripping heaviness of an especially bad summer, idly looking down the caravan line for Tia's dark hair—as if Tia would always be on a caravan simply because they'd met on one.

Rien had no idea where she lived, where she went, what she did.

And if she had seen Tia . . . You were right, she would have had to say. They would sit side by side while the sun turned Tia's hair to fire and Rien still wouldn't quite let her legs dangle off the edge, even though she'd know deep down that it wasn't really falling she was afraid of.

The caravan stopped in Rourk and Rien disembarked; this was her destination. *The fortune-teller in Rourk will give you a gift,* the Prophecy had said. Rien didn't want a gift, and she had more than enough fortune telling in her life. But—she thought— it didn't make sense to turn down a gift; and anyway, she had nowhere else to be.

Rourk was bedecked with ribbons, its windowsills set with fruit and wine, its front doors all crooked open. Rien thought for a moment that this was her gift, but that was foolish; such hospitality was intended for someone far more important than she.

The fortune-teller had birdlike eyes and tiny hands that held Rien's own tightly. Her thumbs stroked Rien's wrists as if she were precious.

"It's so good you've come," she said, smiling at Rien too closely, too sweetly. She touched the side of Rien's face with her smooth fingers and Rien shivered. "So good you've finally come. Wait here; I have something for you."

She disappeared, not further inside but out the front door. Something rose in Rien, fear or agitation; she wanted to leave. I could find Tia, she thought, all of a sudden. I could look for her.

But she didn't move. She was waiting on a Prophesized gift; her patience was infinite.

She stood when the door opened. She turned around to face it, bracing herself, not sure why.

"You must meet Rien," said the fortune-teller, ushering someone in behind her. A man, tall, lean, in a blue suit with a golden flame over his heart. Rien stared at his suit, at that golden flame, and felt the first spark catch in the dry prairie, the first smoke spin out over the grass.

"This is Rien," the fortune-teller said, gesturing. "And this, of course . . . "

Rien looked up and met the Governor's eyes. It was only a

moment; she barely had time to register his face, no time at all to decide if she liked it. Certainly no time for any stronger emotion.

Then a Prophecy boomed out, loud and strong, not a whisper at all: *Your love will last a lifetime, strong and deep.*

Rien's breath froze in the back of her throat.

"Oh, it's destiny!" the fortune-teller gushed, and Rien looked at her sharply, the glee that suffused her expression, the shrewdness in her eyes. Her stomach heaved. Was this her destiny, then? Was this his destiny? The Governor wasn't Prophecy-touched; the Universe couldn't tell *him* what to do.

But she—

She remembered Harsted, Picyute, Evenat, Slie—the Governor had just passed through, the towns were abuzz with it. She had never seen the Governor before; she had always been a step behind him, a shadow nipping at his heels.

Only she was old enough to marry now. Just a month ago, she had turned eighteen. And the fortune-teller had been waiting to meet her. And here they were, she and the Governor, with a Prophecy splitting open above them like a raincloud. And a wife could tell a husband what to do, after all. Nothing wrong with sensible suggestions. No shame in good advice.

The Governor was staring at her, shocked. But Rien saw him look at her more closely, saw him intrigued, saw him interested. And then he smiled at her, and her heart quickened. Was it love? Was it fear? "That was a rather dramatic announcement," he said ruefully, and she couldn't help but laugh. He had beautiful eyes, she noticed reluctantly. Thoughtful eyes. The whole shape of him seemed right.

"Rien, was it?" He reached out to shake her hand but held it instead, and the fortune-teller pressed her own hands to her heart and sighed, and Rien shivered but she didn't pull away. She didn't move at all.

You're a toy in Prophecy's hands, she reminded herself, but the words didn't prick her heart like she meant them to. Wasn't love like that, after all? And wasn't the Governor the best of men, changing everything? Everyone she met had told her of his brilliance. Rien felt like she was sitting at the edge of the boxcar, legs tucked tight, arms wrapped round. Safe. She might as well love him, she realized. Their love would last a lifetime, strong and deep. Could she ask for more?

The Governor glanced around at the fortune-teller's sitting room and then back at her. "Would you like to take a walk?" he asked, still holding Rien's hand, still smiling. He was curious. She was drowning.

"If you ever refuse . . ."

"I would love to," Rien said, but at the hollow sound of her own voice she shuddered. This wasn't the edge of the boxcar at all, she realized—this was lying on the tracks, bleeding and bruised, thinking she was safe just because she couldn't fall any further. Every time she let the Universe redirect her she gave something of herself away, and now the last bits of her were leaking out, her last free breaths were leaving her lungs, and the Governor would take her heart too if she let him.

Suddenly there was a voice inside her, bigger than everything else, demanding her attention. Not the Universe, not the Governor, not the fortune-teller. Not even Tia's voice, this time. Rien's own voice surged up inside her, shaping a prophecy, hoping it was true.

You're not so beat you can't get up. You're not so lost you can't find your own way.

She yanked her hand back, shaking her head. They wouldn't be taking a walk. Finally, finally, Rian had something else she needed to do. And there was somewhere else—with someone else—that she desperately needed to be.

The Gold Chain

Lucy Stone

Lucy Stone is a freelance writer, lexicographer, and mother of one. Her work has appeared in Dreamforge Magazine, All Worlds Wayfarer, Electric Spec, BFS Horizons, Unfading Daydream, Every Day Fiction, Flash Fiction Magazine, Tigershark, and Between These Shores. She has also completed a lavish, meandering Harry Potter fanfic entitled Sympathetic Magic. Her major preoccupations are folklore, romance, and mental illness. Her stories contain many villains, but the ultimate one is usually despair, and she will fight it with every word she writes – even prepositions. She can be found on her website www.lucystonewriter.com, and on Twitter @LucyStoneWriter.

The chain was hanging, suspended from the ceiling of the wood-shed, disappearing between the boards of the roof. Khane had been stooping down to gather firewood for the stove when she had felt its cool weight drop onto the back of her neck. For a moment, she had thought--but it couldn't be. Dead was dead, unless he was a dibbuk. And even dibbuks required someone else's body to walk around in.

She straightened up, and the cool thing draped around her, slipping down the front of her dress. That was when she realized it was a gold chain, thick and heavy and well-made, with links she could have poked her fingers through. Even in the dim glow of her lantern, it was glinting fiercely, as if it was hungry for all the light it could get.

She knew at once what to do. Sonye had told her.

Don't blink. Don't stand there gawping at your good luck. Such miracles happen sometimes, at the close of the Sabbath, though there are fewer nowadays.

Without a word, Khane knelt down, spread her apron, and began gathering the chain into it, pulling it down as if she were milking a cow. She worked with perfect absorption, not even answering when Velvl called her from the kitchen door.

Of course, the stories of such miracles always ended with somebody walking in and causing the good luck to depart--or someone insisting on re-counting the stock, going over the books, trying to discover the source of their good fortune.

Khane knew not to do that. She seized it very firmly with both hands and gathered it into her apron. She had received misfortune blankly enough.

The whole family was at the kitchen door now, calling into the garden. Her stomach growled for the borscht and potatoes, but she didn't move. She watched the gold chain coiling in her apron like a whirlpool. It must have hypnotized her a little, because there was definitely a shock--a spell to be broken--when the ceiling-board above her creaked. It was as if someone were re-distributing their weight, shifting from foot to foot. A fine dusting of snow slipped down and turned to moisture on her fingers.

That was when it occurred to her to be suspicious of the gift. It was also when the gift ran out. She had been leaning most of her weight on the chain as she pulled it down, and now she suddenly fell forwards, as the last of it slipped from the ceiling and clinked onto the floor. Still, the boards above her shifted. Still, the snow feathered down between the cracks and beaded on her skin like sweat.

It was him. Masquerading as a miracle. That had always been his way.

Khane looked down at the gold in her apron and wanted to recoil from it, as if it was a bright, poisonous snake. How was he on the roof? Whose body had he got into?

Very slowly, without causing the gold in her skirts to give a single clink, she reached for the axe propped up against the wood-pile.

He had been a great scholar at the Yeshiva--a student of the Kabbalah. Could he have made a golem? The stories said that the golem of Vilna had been able to walk the rooftops, leap across them in a single bound, walk into the river and gather fish for the Sabbath by calling to them in their own language.

Perhaps Moyshele had made a golem and given it instructions before he died--not to walk the sea-bed or protect the Jewish people, but to hound her. It would be like his pettiness.

There was no more motion. There hadn't been, she realized, for a minute--perhaps two. But now it occurred to her to wonder why Velvl and the others hadn't gone on calling for her.

She got up, spilling gold out of her skirts. She thought she saw it writhing long after it had settled--as if it really *was* a snake.

She knew there was nobody to defend her. Velvl hated violence, even if he was still alive, and Sonye--but her mind clamped down on that thought before she could think it. Nothing had happened to Sonye. Nothing *could* happen to Sonye. She was too wise and wily; she knew the stories of the world too well.

She backed out of the door, still clutching the axe firmly in her hand. She would have to keep facing the roof. If it really was Moyshele, it wouldn't do to turn her back on him. And besides, she didn't want to see the door of her house standing open, and wonder about what she would find inside.

So she backed slowly down the garden path until the snow-covered slats of the roof came into view.

He was crouched on top of them, smiling. He looked like Velvl--and, for the barest skin of a second, she was fooled. But then she saw the way he carried himself, the insolence in his expression, the restlessness of his movements, and she recognized her dead husband in her new husband's face.

In life, he had made a career as a balshem, a wonder-worker. She knew every one of his tricks, but had never given him away, though each one had built up her contempt for him, brick by brick.

He had once painted a cat in tar and feathers and sewn it up inside the mattress of a girl who was supposed to be possessed by a dibbuk. When the girl and her family had seen him driving a black, yowling creature out of her feather-bed, they had declared him to be a wonder-worker, and showered him with złotych.

Mostly, he had sold amulets and talismans for women hoping to get pregnant. Sometimes, he had winked at these women and told them he could help them by more earthly means if they cared to come back after sunset. He had used squibs and effervescent powders, chanted garbled phrases from the Torah and the Kabbalah. He had been a degenerate.

If this was another trick, it was a good one. Or had he finally--after his death--become the real thing?

His shoulders were white with snow, as if the dust of ages had settled on him. And, even as her throat seized up, Khane was still lucid enough to say:

"And to think--all that time I thought it was going to be a light-hearted tale about someone stumbling in on a miracle and causing it to take flight."

He tilted his head in an eager, bird-like way, and spoke with the voice of Moyshele, even though he was using Velvl's tongue, and Velvl's vocal cords.

"Always a story, isn't it? Even now, you're thinking about how to moralize this, how to sum it up neatly."

Khane shrugged. She could feel the warmth of the open door at her back. Had the others gone home? Please God, they were not lying there dead in front of the unlit stove.

She tried not to think about the fact that she had an extra life to consider. She was pregnant--although so far she had felt this, not as a quickening of life within her, but as a mild form of sea-sickness. Perhaps that made sense. You had a sea inside you when you were with child, and a little, ship-wrecked mariner, ready to be washed up on the shore of the world. She wasn't sure she had any love for the mariner yet, but she didn't like to think of it dying.

She didn't know whether it was Velvl's or Moyshele's. The transition from husband to husband had been that fast--indecently fast, some of her neighbours had said. But she'd had her eye on that simple, honest-faced shoemaker throughout all her troubles: a man who didn't pretend, a man who was as gentle with his loved ones as he was with his work--and, best of all, a man who had Sonye for his mother.

"You are a dibbuk?" she said, in the most matter-of-fact tone she could muster. "I should have known you wouldn't lie quietly. You never did."

He leapt down from the roof, landing lightly in the snow. She could see his footprints--the perfect impressions of Velvl's well-made soles--as he walked forwards.

Khane knew her options were limited. Only a rabbi could cast out a dibbuk. You had to say holy words, you had to be sanctified.

"What do you want?" she said.

"You. You come with me to my grave, dead or alive. You met me under the wedding canopy, you can meet me under the earth."

Khane shrugged again. "It's an improvident waste to keep a woman from living just because her husband happens to be dead."

Though he *had* kept her from living, she realized. She might just as well have been the golem of Vilna, she felt so cold. It was only when she and Sonye sat beside the stove swapping stories, their eyes glittering like live coals, that she felt alive.

"Your husband is not dead," said the dibbuk. He let just enough of Velvl's voice creep into this pronouncement to make her hesitate. "He's right here before you, body and spirit. If the body and the spirit answer to different names, what of that? You met them both under the wedding canopy, at one time or another."

Khane swung the axe, but he caught it in mid-air and wrenched it out of her hands, with the effortless strength of a golem.

She didn't react. Her hopes had not been high in any case.

"What are you doing here?" she said. "Why aren't you in the city charging five złotych for admission, now you can really work the wonders you boasted of all your life?"

He answered breezily enough, though his teeth were set.

"Because real wonders don't look like wonders on the stage. Real possession isn't accompanied by fireworks or a dramatic dimming of the lights."

Khane thought about this. She supposed Velvl's eyes were not gleaming with demonic fire--his voice sounded like Moyshele's, but perhaps it was only because she knew them so well that she could tell the difference.

"I could have had the real thing," he went on, "and been ignored all my life, if I'd chosen to. But I wanted to make an impression on people."

"You made an impression on me," she said, barely parting her lips.

It was a reproach, not a grudging admission, but still, it kindled something in him. There was a glimmer of excitement in his expression. It would have been unnoticeable on Moyshele's face, but Velvl's was so open.

Khane felt a kick of bitterness that made her want to laugh. He wanted to impress her. Was that why he was walking? Was that his unfinished business? She didn't think she could bear to feign admiration for him, even if it would save her life. Much better to moulder with him under the ground, silently hating him, as she had in life.

But there was a grain of comfort there, though she had to look quite hard to unearth it. If he wanted her admiration, then it would do no good to possess her. What he wanted had to be given freely, or it would have no value at all.

"You will follow me to the graveyard and dig yourself in."

"Digging is work," said Khane solemnly. "I am not allowed to work on the Sabbath."

The dibbuk hissed through his teeth, and almost at the same moment, she heard the clink of the gold chain. It had snaked out of the open door of the wood-shed, and now she felt its chill on her leg, inching up her skirts, binding her ankles together.

Still, she didn't bow her head. She was grateful it was no worse. Knowing him, it might have been.

"I'll check on the others before I go anywhere with you," she said. She knew she was in no position to be making demands; she knew she couldn't convince him she wasn't afraid of him, but she would go to her grave trying--or, if necessary, to his.

He made a mocking gesture of assent, and Khane shifted in her chains, trying to work them loose enough for her to turn and walk. In the end, she settled for turning, with a little, clinking jump.

The door stood open, as she had feared. Velvl was not inside, of course, but Sonye was standing at the table, mid-way through stirring the sorrel soup. Leye and Miriam were seated on either side of her, their hands steepled in front of them, as if in prayer.

Khane waited a few seconds, but she knew, somehow, that there would be no change.

She tried to work her ankles free of the chain. She wanted to touch them. If they felt warm beneath her fingertips, then at least she would know they were still alive.

"They're not aware of time passing," said Moyshele. With his usual nervous energy, he had come to stand beside her, and was now shifting from foot to foot, glaring at the frozen figures, as if he envied their serenity.

Khane looked round at the other lighted windows of the shtetl. There was no movement. In the attic of the Weinreichs' house, she could see *Bubbe* Rokhl in her rocking chair, not rocking. Yankl was standing on the steps, frozen in the act of stamping snow off his boots. Khane had a wild, stupid urge to throw her shawl around him.

They were not asleep. Somehow, Moyshele had put them outside of time.

Yet she could see why he was hunching his shoulders with

annoyance. There was no spectacle, no audience. Real wonders didn't look as good as carefully stage-managed tricks.

It made her think of the desperation you would need to be a dibbuk--to resist the steady, quiet pull of death. It would be like swimming upstream every second.

He had always been that desperate, she realized. He had lived his life in a flare of desperation, planning wonders, making speeches, dipping in and out of books for just long enough to glean impressive-sounding phrases from them.

And now he had all these powers, but not his name, not his face. He could perform wonders, but not as himself. He could use Velvl's voice to proclaim his true identity, but what then? The rabbi would cast him out--and, even if people remembered, they would remember him as the villain, not the wonder-worker. He'd be on the wrong side of history. They both knew what that was like.

She had been surprised to learn he wasn't in Gehenna, but perhaps he *was.*

"When you are beneath the earth with me," he said, "I'll let them go. Your shoe-maker too."

He blew on his hands, restless and discontented. He couldn't possibly be cold--dibbuks couldn't feel the cold--but his earthly habits were ingrained too deep. No wonder he was walking.

"I think you'll agree it's a generous offer, in the circumstances."

That was when Khane realized that she had seen the gold chain before. It was one of the bright, tinny stage-props he had used in his shows. She had kept it in a chest in the attic, along with the jars and powders and grimoires and other useless junk she had inherited when he'd died.

She set her jaw and wrenched her ankles apart. The chain dug deep into her flesh, but it still broke.

The dibbuk pressed Velvl's face into a smile. "I had you fooled, though, didn't I?"

"And what was the point of that?" said Khane. "When you can possess people and stop time and animate inanimate objects, where is the need for passing tin off as gold?"

"It's more eye-catching," he said. He had clenched his fists, but was keeping them close at his sides. He was still smiling. "I've missed this."

"You'll have it for a grand total of three minutes if you force me to share your grave with you."

"No," he said, shaking Velvl's head. "You'll walk with me. I know another restless spirit when I see one."

***

She walked after him to the graveyard by the synagogue, feeling the snow settle on her shoulders. For a long time now, it hadn't bothered her. Some people reacted violently to the cold--shivering and stamping and chattering their teeth--but Khane had always felt it as a comfort. It settled on her shoulders now like Sonye's hands.

There were no endings, Sonye said. Only beginnings somewhere else. And the Jews of long-dead generations lived on through their stories, and could never really come to harm.

Khane had her doubts on this matter, though she hadn't voiced them. She had long suspected that stories existed to serve the purpose of the people telling them. In Brzezany, outside the ghetto--where Moyshele's work had occasionally taken them--she had been known as the pretty Jewess, with eyes that could steal your soul away.

And that had not been the worst of it. She knew the fictions the Gentiles told themselves to get out of paying their debts, to make themselves feel better about rape and murder. That was why it was so important for her people to tell stories of their own: to preserve an image of themselves as something other than grasping money-lenders and servants of the devil, just in case the Gentiles got their way.

She had never really thought she was whiling away the time, when she'd sat beside the stove, swapping stories with Sonye. She had known it was important, that she was interceding on behalf of her people, just like the rabbis--just like the cantors in the synagogue.

Could a story save her now? She knew what he wanted. Could she make him believe he'd already got it? Not her admiration--that wouldn't keep him satisfied for long--but the admiration of the whole world, or at least a chance of winning it?

"Everybody wept for you," she said, watching his back as they walked.

"Hah," he spat. "They wept for how difficult their lives were going to be without me." He turned, and gave her one of his horrible, sarcastic snarls. "And you leapt into the shoe-maker's bed before I was even cold."

"I had to provide for our child," she said.

Again, Velvl's open face betrayed him. His lips parted with

surprise. She could see him calculating--how long he had been dead, how far gone she could be, with no bulge showing at her belly.

"It's his," he said flatly.

"I haven't bled in four months," said Khane. "It is not his."

The dibbuk didn't speak.

"He'll have your name, of course," she said. "That's only proper."

She paused to let this sink in, then added:

"He will be a great man. Perhaps he will even look like you."

His face was still tight with scorn, but she could see the greed in it. Something with his name--maybe even his face--could go on after him, and win all the admiration he was craving.

Would that mean he could rest? He was phenomenally selfish, but then this new creature *would* be himself, in all the shallow ways that mattered to him.

He clenched his fists once or twice, as if in indecision, and then he gave a little sigh, and all the tension in his body slackened. It was like rolling out pastry--all the bumps and wrinkles smoothed themselves out under the weight of this realization. Something with his name would go on living.

He staggered. And Moyshele's stagger became Velvl's fall.

She couldn't explain how she knew that it was suddenly Velvl-- his eyes were closed, his face devoid of all expression--but it was. The dibbuk had gone.

Khane staggered too. She fell on her knees in the snow, but couldn't feel the cold soaking through her skirts. She would have liked to let her shoulders droop, and sob uncontrollably into her hands, but it would take a while for her to let her guard down. She had been reigning herself in so tightly.

Besides, she wasn't perfectly convinced that she was safe. She could see motion at the windows of the nearest houses now. There was even a snatch of music, though it sounded tinny and discordant, as if the notes were being stretched out of their proper shape. Perhaps time was coming back in little bursts, and was having difficulty finding its rhythm.

She couldn't believe he was really gone. She couldn't believe she had really tricked the trickster.

Perhaps she hadn't. Perhaps the child *was* his, and would grow to be just like him--or worse, perhaps dibbuks could inhabit unborn children, and her little, ship-wrecked mariner would turn out to be her worst nightmare. She knew enough about motherhood to suspect that this might be the case, whether her child was possessed or not.

There were no endings, Sonye said. Only beginnings somewhere else. Khane wasn't sure what kind of story this was the beginning of--only that she knew a lot of stories, and could always find a way to thrive within them. Besides, she had Sonye, who knew even more.

She got up, seized Velvl by the legs, and began to drag him home through the snow.

The Artist

Koji A. Dae

Koji A. Dae is an American living longterm in Bulgaria. When not writing or wrangling her kids she can be found hunting down second hand bargains. She has work forthcoming or published with Short Edition, ParABnormal Magazine, Lucent Dreaming, and Honey & Lime Literary. You can find out more about her at kojiadae.ink

Karla Becker had a habit of talking to her crystals as she programmed them. The constant, indiscernible chatter earned her the furthest workstation from the door and stares from her coworkers. She didn't mind. When she worked, the world beyond her crystals faded. Completely immersed, she didn't notice Emerson standing in her cubicle until he stood directly behind her.

"Becker, I need to..."

The crystal Karla held—somewhere between purple and green, like a darkening bruise—skidded out of her hand and across her station. It clinked as it hit two other finger-sized crystals, and Karla cut off Emerson off with a swear.

"Emerson, can't you knock?" The fallen crystal faded to obsidian black, and its bruising seeped into the two crystals it touched.

"Are those infected now?" He nodded at the crystals, all three black and useless.

"They are." Sweeping the crystals into the center of her workstation, she took the metal probes off the one she had dropped. "What did you need?"

"I came to talk to you about this. It's got to stop."

She traced the edges of a crystal. Several large chips on each smooth face made it unusable for anything other than her experiments. Perfect crystals, when programmed to the correct frequencies, could dig through the caverns, extracting minerals and expanding to create rooms or entire buildings. This one wouldn't even be able to make non-responsive furniture. "This is important work, and you know it."

He picked up a crystal and held it close to his eye as he turned it over. The light reflected off the glossy surface, but beneath the sheen, the structure of the crystal had disappeared into inky oblivion.

"What I know is this obsession will get you fired."

She turned to face him. "Have you heard something?"

He placed a hand on her tense shoulder and despite herself she leaned into the touch. "I've more than heard. I've been told. This is your last warning, Becker. You've gotten a lot of leeway because of your breakthrough, but that was almost two years ago. You can't ride that success forever. They don't want you wasting time on this project, and they don't want you destroying any more crystals."

"I don't use viable crystals." She shrugged his hand away.

"Doesn't matter. They want it to stop. It's time to get back to real work. You're an amazing architect. Go back to that, not whatever this is."

"Just because it can't be marketed and sold," Karla grumbled, "They don't understand."

"Understand what?"

His eyes softened and Karla almost told him, but her lips refused to move. Even Emerson wouldn't believe her. Not if she told him the crystals were alive.

***

Like every day in the underground city of New Ironwood, the weather was perfect, the crystal architecture immaculate. The high ceiling of the atrium was the pale yellow of sparkling wine, the columns dusted with a pinch of pink. Karla rushed across the open space, ignoring the imported trees, keeping her head down and navigating away from groups of people by avoiding their colorful slippers.

Looking up wouldn't make a difference. Almost all of them were deep into their alternative realities, talking with friends on different levels, playing immersive games. No one would have noticed she was there, seen her tear-streaked face, or asked what was wrong.

Once she got to the small tunnel on the other side of the cavern, she dragged her fingertips along the smooth, cool surface of the crystal walls that curved up into the ceiling. She would miss the curated colors of her city: the iridescent shimmering of her pink flat, the white of her laboratory. She wouldn't have chosen such a dull gray for the entrance tunnel. But Karla didn't choose the colors. She had just made it possible for the people who did.

When she discovered how to separate rooms from the central color grid, people called her an artist. Because of her, citizens could set one room to green while another shimmered in sea-foam blue. That's the kind of breakthrough her employers demanded. Correction. Former employers.

"Name?" The gate attendant barely looked up from his tablet where he pushed tiny colored dots together into shapes.

"Karla Becker." She said her name quietly.

The attendant's stubby finger stopped in the middle of a move. The screen flashed a bright red warning as he peeled his eyes from the game, losing a life to assess Karla's face. With Connect living in everyone's brain, linking them to the people they wanted to be with instead of the ones they were forced to be near, eye contact with strangers was a rarity. She blushed under the gate attendant's scrutiny.

"You're moving out?" He nodded at the self-driving pallet humming behind her. It was stacked with plastic bins and awaiting its next order.

"Yeah."

"But you're our artist!" He waved at the walls, the podium, and the floor—all a dull gray to match the ancient concrete of the Ironwood tunnel.

The rogue muscle at the back of her jaw—the one that kept sending her to the dentist—pulled tight. He claimed her as if he knew her, as if she belonged to the city just because the results of her equations covered their walls. But they didn't value her work enough to let her keep her job at the architectural center or her flat in the underground city.

She let his objection drop between them. She was done reassuring people in New Ironwood.

***

The Ironwood tunnel, connecting the underground city to its namesake above ground, was from the days before crystal architecture. A layer of grime coated the concrete walls with streaks of black. The train lurched out of the tunnel, its slow rhythm loosening the muscle in her jaw.

No longer sheltered by the crystal caverns of New Ironwood, Karla cowered against the pleather seat. Orange-gray clouds stretched across the open sky.

The train stopped at the poorly maintained station. With an expert twitch of her mind, Karla accessed her Connect and commanded her pallet to follow her off the train. She pulled up a map and turned on the navigation to the address the real estate agent had sent her.

A path, Karla's favorite shade of dark purple with lilac specks, lit up in front of her. Trying to ignore the cracked pavement, Karla followed the sparkles. The visual overlay smoothed the rough edges of the neglected city, softening reality.

"You're late." A clipped voice forced Karla to look up just as her Connect informed her she had arrived at Tesla Coffee Shop. She parked the pallet next to the patio and flicked off the navigation. The purple path vanished, leaving only the dismal concrete and a cafe filled with people dressed in layered, inefficient fabrics with folds and pleats, buckles and chains. The depressing buildings seemed to grow out of the ground. No, not grow. They were stacked on top and a breath away from crumbling back to it.

The woman staring at her was sporting the pragmatic fashion of New Ironwood. The neck-to-ankle, skin-tight therm suit put Karla at ease. Her blonde hair was pinned in a tight bun, ankle-high leather boots her only extravagance. Of course slippers wouldn't provide enough protection against the roughness of the outer city.

The blonde's eyes seemed to stroke Karla's face as she waited.

Karla flushed beneath the scrutiny. But looking around, the other patrons of the cafe shared a similar intimacy. They exchanged words and thoughts while looking right at each other. The only person who had looked at Karla that way before was Emerson—once when they had slept together and again when he had fired her. The woman's attention was steady, as if she actually cared what Karla would say or do next. Drawn in by the promise of her gaze, Karla leaned closer to the blonde.

"I'm Karla Becker." Karla offered her hand to the woman, wondering if her name held as much weight outside the crystal city. For the first time, she hoped it did. Part of her wanted to keep the woman's eyes on her.

After a brief handshake, the woman sat at the table, bringing a tablet to life with her fingerprint. "I'm Tybee. Let's find you an apartment, shall we?"

Tybee tapped a picture of Karla on the screen. Emerson had taken it years ago, while Karla stood proudly in the center of her lab, surrounded by the latest crystal tech—machines she had helped tweak and improve and would never have access to again. The picture faded, replaced by a gallery of drab rooms, each of them with peeling paint, cracked tiling, and suspicious gray growths in the corners. Karla's eyes darted over the rooms and back to Tybee's perfectly painted lips.

"Those are my options?"

"I'm afraid so." Tybee didn't even try to sound optimistic. "You're on Basic Income now. You qualify for a basic apartment, either a studio or a small one bedroom. If you care about quality, start with the smaller units."

"It doesn't matter. Just pick one for me." Karla's room in New

Ironwood had been small, too, but beautiful in a way concrete could never compete with.

Tybee's professionalism softened, and she reached across the table to touch the back of Karla's hand. Karla swallowed to keep her breath from quickening.

"It's not so bad out here," Tybee said, "Many people on Basic Income sublet rooms in better apartments from those earning full incomes."

Tybee withdrew her fingers and tapped on her tablet to show Karla a picture of a neat bedroom, bathed in orangish-brown sunlight. It was clean and painted a soft cream color.

"This is my spare room."

***

Karla's plastic bins ended up in Tybee's spare room, and a week later her body landed in Tybee's bed, clinging to Tybee like a lifeboat in a wild sea. After, Tybee laid her head on Karla's shoulder and snuggled into her.

Karla was struck by their nakedness. Just skin and racing energy. She waited for Tybee to flip on her Connect, to escape the intimacy and vulnerability the way Emerson had.

But Tybee didn't reach for her implant. Instead she murmured, "You're an artist."

For once Karla didn't shudder under the title. "That's what everyone says. But I'm just an architect. All math and equations, no real imagination."

Tybee closed Karla's hand in her own, holding it above her lazy beating heart. "No, I've felt it. I know."

***

An old desk, made from pressed particle-board and coated in light brown laminate, sat next to the bed in Karla's new room. She opened a case and let her fingertip trace the shape of the large, inky-black crystal at the top before taking out one of the clear, thumb-sized crystals from the foam packing. She set the crystal on the desk, collapsed into a padded chair, and considered it.

Technically, she shouldn't have had raw crystals, but she had the case checked out when they let her go. Her boss said they were letting her keep her pride by not officially firing her, as if that was enough. But it wasn't. So she hadn't returned the suitcase of sample crystals or the portable crystal programmer. Most of the crystals were chunky and mottled. Worthless. The architectural center probably didn't miss them.

Karla took the small, boxy computer out of one of her bins and set it next to the mostly smooth, sharp-edged crystal. With deft hands she found the two deepest nooks in the crystal and rubbed the sticky diodes against them until the plastic wiring molded to almost imperceptible lines in the rocks.

Her fingerprint, held against the glass screen of the mini-computer, beckoned the programmer to life. Three taps of her forefinger unlocked the diagnostics program.

The crystal was well-formed with few imperfections, a good candidate for several programs. Karla could turn it into a cavernous chamber with perfect acoustics or a three-room office center. With a bit of custom coding it might even serve as a medical clinic. But as she stared at it, a certainty that it could be something more grew in her. She just didn't know what.

With a press of the rice-like button behind her ear, Karla fell into her Connect profile. Full immersion. Old Ironwood faded as easily and completely as New Ironwood always had. Karla thought her way down levels of files, spiraling into herself with graceful weightlessness.

At the bottom of the program was a gray folder with no label—a gift from one of her mind-architect colleagues. The experimental interface allowed her to run interactive crystal simulations. She selected the folder and was immediately overwhelmed with the size of the crystal she had scanned. It was bigger than the diagnostic had estimated, at least ten rooms, stacked in three levels.

Karla entered the first room—perfectly cubed, flawless surfaces. She reached towards a wall, forgetting it was just a simulation, and felt humming vibrations echo through her body.

The old crystal-architects, who had built New Ironwood and whose programs Karla had studied for years, tended to underestimate the potential of crystals. But Karla suspected working with the natural vibrations of these hard creatures would yield better results than forcing them into humanity's frequencies. She let the crystal's low hum fill her, echo back out of her until she was sick with the vibrations. Only then did she try to match its drone with an echo in her own throat.

Her hum rose in pitch until she found the major seventh chord. She pitched it down a half-step, pressing it into a minor chord that conflicted with the base note of the room. Karla pressed her hand harder against the wall until she felt a slow cracking. The room was isolated.

Her hand—her real one—flew to her ear, turning off the program and returning her to reality. On the desk the crystal lay in two pieces, one smaller than the nail on her pinkie finger. Karla picked up the tiny piece.

"What do you want to be?" she whispered to the crystal.

She took several passes over several days to shave off a delicate sliver of the crystal. By the time she got it to less than a hundredth of a gram, she knew it intimately enough to whip out a program by hand, the nodes pulsing electricity into the tiny piece, singing it into a sculpture.

***

At first her sculptures were crude. Karla had to break into an abandoned apartment building and pull apart the plasterboard to dig out some copper wiring. She stretched it into smaller probes, fit for her tiny crystals. After that excursion, the sculptures bloomed—soft edges, hard lines, perfect symmetry.

Her pieces sold well. She started with simple geometric shapes before expanding into flowers. Poppies were her favorite, and she loved the final push to make them glow dark red, their delicate stems a deep green. With time she took commissions: models of a boat, an old car from the days when people drove personal automobiles, a replica of a loved one.

For Tybee's birthday, Karla gave her a bust cut to showcase the way Tybee had appeared the first day they met. Her hair and skin were clear, but her lips and eyelids shimmered with liquid red.

Tybee looked like a different woman as she placed the sculpture on a shelf in their living room. Her hair was loose rather than pinned up these days, and she rarely wore makeup. Tybee's relaxation reflected Karla's. As Karla shed her attachment to the prim formality of New Ironwood, Tybee descended with her, touching the basic rhythm of the old city.

"You're doing well with these sculptures. You can afford your own apartment now."

"Are you trying to kick me out?" Karla wrapped her arms around Tybee's waist.

"No. But you can move back to New Ironwood. Isn't that what you want?"

Karla pulled back, a laugh dying in her throat. She retreated into her room and returned with the black crystal from her suitcase. The heavy rock clanked against the glass coffee table.

Tybee's blue eyes went wide as she was pulled into the swirling depths of the crystal.

"I've never seen a black crystal."

"Not many people have. This is what I was working on when they fired me."

"It's beautiful."

"It is, but to get that rich, full black, I unlock the structure of the crystal. I amplify its internal vibrations and break down its compartments. I release its essence."

Tybee stared at the crystal, obviously overwhelmed by it. But Karla could tell she didn't understand.

"They said my project was worthless. Once a crystal turns black, they can't program it. Worse, its disease, as they called it, spreads to every crystal it comes in contact with. They all turn this color and stop responding to programming. My boss told me I needed to stop trying to figure out what was happening and get back to working on structure. Things we can use. Things they can control and sell."

Karla looked out the window. The people below moved in chaotic paths, their billowing clothes flowing in the summer breeze.

They swirled with a freedom the people of New Ironwood had long forgotten in their perfectly structured city.

"I could have stayed. All I had to do was stop working on my project. But I couldn't." Karla ran the pad of her finger over the black crystal as if she was petting a fragile animal.

"Why not?" Tybee asked, reaching out to run her hand over the strange crystal, bumping against Karla's fingers.

"Because..." Karla hesitated, unsure if she should tell Tybee the truth. "They're alive. When they're clear, they're dormant. But I think I've found a way to release their natural state."

"You mean, they're conscious?" Tybee pulled back her finger.

Karla shrugged. "In a way. I wanted to figure out what I could do once I learned to speak with the crystals. The sculptures are just the first step. But I want to learn how to communicate with the black ones."

Karla waited for Tybee to laugh or turn away. But she didn't. Instead, she ran her hand up Karla's bare arm and cupped it behind her neck, drawing Karla into a slow and tender kiss. "You will, my artist."

***

The city of Old Ironwood commissioned a sculpture from Karla—a giant Ironwood tree in the central park. They wanted a testament to the city that would remain green year round. They supplied her with additional copper and a larger programming console that allowed her to tweak the individual leaves of the massive sculpture.

After weeks of work, more math than singing, she removed the copper probes from the sculpture and her crew stripped away the sheets hanging around her project. A small crowd cheered as the crystal leaves fluttered on delicate stems in the breeze.

"Magnificent!" The mayor tipped Karla with a hundred-year-old bottle of brandy.

After the crowd left, Karla and Tybee sat under Karla's tree, sipping from the bottle until they were giddy drunk on the sweet liquid. By then Karla had traded out her therms for flowing cotton skirts and crop tops pinned tight beneath a variety of vests. She loved the way the vests clung to her ribcage, hugging her, and laughed at how the folds of her skirt spilled over onto Tybee's legs, still covered in therms.

"It's beautiful." Tybee gazed at the glittering leaves. "So alive."

"Yeah, it is." Karla pulled a small black crystal from the pouch at her waist and considered it. She gave Tybee what would have been a wicked grin if the brandy hadn't turned it lopsided. "Want to know a secret?"

She pressed the crystal to the base of the tree, fitting it into the hollow between two roots. The shimmering black inked out of the small crystal, spreading up the tree trunk and out to the leaves.

Tybee backed away from the black tree that swirled like a galaxy above her. "The mayor's going to be pissed."

Karla stood, the white lace at the hem of her skirt tickling her ankles. She placed her hand on the trunk of the tree.

Her lips parted, and she curled her tongue against the roof of her mouth. A low, wild song grew out of her belly, through her vocal chords. She constricted her throat and sent a forceful drone out her mouth and nose. The sound was both high and low, two separate notes bouncing off each other. Slowly, color returned to the tree. The canopy became even more vibrant than it had been, the leaves a thousand shades of green at once, as the blackness dripped down the trunk like a waterfall running over rocks, leaving behind streaks of white and gray and brown.

Karla picked up the black crystal, pocketing it in her leather hip bag.

"Your eyes." Tybee stumbled back from Karla.

Karla shook her head, closed her eyes. When she opened them the black had gone from them and Tybee stepped forward again.

"My employers were right, the black crystals won't be programmed. But they are sympathetic to exchange."

"You talked to it?" Tybee's eyebrows wrinkled into a sharp point above her nose. "This could change the way they build cities."

Karla caressed the smooth crystal in her pouch. "Not just cities. These crystals hold ancient knowledge. We could build above ground, strip the minerals from the air. The black crystals could take us into space, if we let them, protected in and guided by living ships."

"You've got to tell someone. Your employers? The government?"

Karla snorted. "They don't want to hear that the crystals are alive. They want to think it's all math and science and the will of man. Do you know how much longer it takes to build a relationship with a crystal and learn to talk with it instead of writing some code and overpowering it with electrical impulses? Who cares that they could eventually do more. Right now it would cut into their profit margins."

"And you'll just let them go on believing the crystals are inert?"

"Nope." Karla took the last swig of brandy, her face contorting under the weight of the alcohol.

She took off towards the New Ironwood tunnel, Tybee trailing a few steps behind. Instead of entering the mouth of the enormous tunnel, Karla hiked her skirt up, held the hem in one hand, and used her free hand to keep herself steady as she scrambled up the rocky slope.

By the time they reached the top of the mountain both women were out of breath. Tybee's therms were cut open around her knees, and Karla's skirt carried twigs in its fabric. But the scramble hadn't sobered them. Karla's reached out to one of the fat crystal columns protruding from the mountain. The columns carried light into the underground city. During one of her rotations it had been her job to keep the short pillars clean. She and Emerson had hiked the hill once a week to wipe down the crystals and spray them with a solution that kept the dust away.

She wondered who had the job now. Some other teenage girl hoping to be the best crystal-architect in the world, no doubt. The girl probably spent her days studying structure and nights dreaming of patterns, finding new ones that weren't really there. If she hadn't been drunk, Karla might have felt sorry for the girl as she placed the black crystal on top of a creamy white pillar.

It took a moment for the color to pass through the protective coating, but the two crystals harmonized and the black color oozed down the white crystal, into the ground. Karla imagined it coating each layer of the city in blackness. Her stark white lab, black now. Her pink room, the green parks, the blue medical offices, all of it black. Her fingers flexed, almost sweeping the crystal off of the pillar, but it was too late to turn back. She ignored the churning in her stomach and pressed the crystal harder into the pillar.

"They'll know it was you," Tybee whispered, taking Karla's free hand.

"Yep, but it doesn't matter. I gave them color, I can take it away." Karla's voice was deeper, and her eyes had changed again.

Shouts already echoed up the mountainside, the harbingers of security forces with guns and handcuffs, coming for Karla.

"But they'll be in darkness. It'll be chaos."

Karla buried her face in her lover's loose hair, breathing in the scent of roses from her shampoo. "This is my gift to them. It's the only way I can make them admit what these crystals really are."

The voices grew closer.

Tybee pulled away, ready to run. "Then you'll turn them back?"

Karla stroked the black column. "No. Then I'll teach the people to sing with them."

Tonghai

Linda H. Codega

Linda is a twenty-something queer millennial living and working in the Hudson Valley. They love fandom, pop culture, sailing, tarot cards, and crying in movie theaters. Their short stories have been published in Luna Station Quarterly, Helios Quarterly, and Dark Moon Digest, among others.

Jian hadn't seen another person in fifty-eight days. She marked each lonely rotation on the inside of her hull with dots made from kelp paste. Fifty-eight wasn't so long.

She slid around the makeshift table, squeezing down a small hall, and opened the door to the boat's deck. She shut the door firmly behind her, checking the seals. Jian stood up to her full height in the cockpit of the *Green Moon*. Surveying the dark sea on all sides, Jian felt the expanse of the Tonghai flowing around her boat. It was familiar, dark and loving. Closing her eyes, the woman took a deep breath, pressing her hands against her torso, finding comfort in the harnesses' webbing across her body.

Her fingers were sure as she clasped the lockjaw on the front of her harness and then on the lifeline. She opened her eyes, moving then across the *Green Moon*. The system was a spider's web of plastigut all across her boat, a precaution against freak waves or unpredictable storms, or Jian's own nerves. Safety accounted for, Jian walked along the deck, one foot after the other. Her feet were rough with calluses, and the alloshark skin she wrapped around her arches every week made it easier for her to keep steady on the often-slick hull.

From the entrance belowdecks it wasn't far to the tiller, and she switched around the locks on the harness, sitting down comfortably. She was still headed West, toward the asterism her ancestors called Tiger King. Something like that. Jian wasn't sure.

The white needle on her onboard compass waved across the marks. The sunsails were still up, glowing faintly with leftover solar from the day. It would be enough to keep her on course, even if the wind didn't pick up in the night.

She shifted over, pressing another button and turning a large dial on the side of the hull, manually pulling up a salinometer. Still toxic. Not sludge, at least, but any fish or kelp she'd try to harvest would be so laden with chem and barriers she'd risk disease just by bringing it on deck. It was the thirtieth day of oceanox water, and Jian's supplies were getting dangerously low.

There was a place—Jian knew, Jian had heard, Jian had been told—in the west, heralded by Tiger King and guarded by the Great Escapements, where there was fresh water. A fount of clean water, not just the not-quite-toxic currents she chased on her solarschooner. Even when the oceanox receded deep below the surface, and the sweetwater rose to the wave's crest in cool weather, she still needed her sifturbines to work through chem and toxisalt to deliver semi-potable water. There wasn't clean water anymore.

Jian pressed her lips together and sat back. The debris ring overhead was continually shifting; a massive clutch of orbiting garbage that sparkled a dusky bronze in the moonlight. Holding her hands up, she compared the constellations tattooed there to the winking stars in the sky, carefully matching them up—*wei–zhao–jiuhe– zhongshan*. She turned her wrists, continuing to draw the asterisms across her tanned skin.

In between her arms, crossing the inked border between the

Supreme Palace and the Heavenly Enclosure, passed a tellerite. Jian dropped her hands quickly, standing up, eyes to the technology flying above her. Her hands shook as she undid the harness. Once free, she darted up the deck like a dolphin, jumping onto the aft mast and scrambling up to watch the tellerite fly overhead.

It had been four hundred and eighty-six days since she last saw a tellerite. They came a long time ago, and starting circling the various latitudes almost immediately. They were...ships, of some kind. There were a thousand different stories.

The massive tellerite above Jian had two large, spinning rings at the front of it, blazing through the sky. On the outside of the rings, a series of white and blue lights flashed, reminding Jian of the messages that large ships sent each other across the Tonghai.

In the center of the ring hovered a catamaran hull, long and segmented like a piece of bamboo with three exact sections. As the boat rocked forward along the wind, Jian could see shimmering threads of silken light connecting the inside of the rings to the segmented craft. At the end of the vehicle, sticking out a long way from the rings guiding the ship, there were three small starburst-shaped propellers that emitted a greenish glow, much like the St. Ulmo's fire that lit up the top of her mast in sparking weather.

The tellerite passed with no indication of having seen Jian's ship. It was orbiting at such a high altitude, that it took nearly an hour for Jian to lose sight of it. She strained her eyes, trying to pick out green fire against the flickering trash and stars. Eventually, she admitted to herself that she could no longer see the strange craft.

Her fingers were numb as she stumbled back to the transom of the boat, her hands trailing along the holds on the deck. Her mind was still on the tellerite as she walked back to the tiller.

She didn't realize that her harness was loose around her chest, that her lockjaw wasn't on a lifeline.

A wave rocked the boat. Jian missed a step and slammed to her knees. She slid off the side of the boat as the *Green Moon* rose up fast on the crest. She caught herself on the outer lifeline, eyes wide with panic. The dark ocean surrounded her. Jian gasped and pulled herself onto the boat, her whole body shaking. She immediately felt the rough prick of poison on her skin.

Jian cursed, stood up quickly and darted into the cockpit. She shucked off her pants to protect her skin from further contact with the poison. Her legs were already starting to get hot and she was sweating behind her knees.

Stumbling belowdecks, Jian used a foot pump to draw purified water into the sink, mindful of the pressure even with her shaking legs. Her breath caught as a spike of pain dug into her calf. She wet a rag and quickly ran it over her legs, sloughing away the ocean's toxisalt. The ocean had turned into a dark acidic compound over the millennia of picking up the afterbirth of a hundred civilizations. The hardened base plasticine of her hull and deck could handle the toxicity, and even nullify the acid to an extent, but her legs were not so tough.

The heat, almost agonizing, continued. Jian grimaced. The rag was covered with her leg hair, seared off at the root. She took a deep breath, angry and afraid. Her heart raced as she centered herself. After she steeled her nerves, Jian wiped her legs down again. This time, burnt-umber skin peeled off. Jian's jaw clenched, a marlin-spike of anger digging into her, just as sharp as the burning sensation on her legs.

Closing her eyes tightly, Jian scrubbed around the outside edge of the chem burns, removing any trace of the grey-green molting that was already starting to show. Infections could spread into the open wound, even from clean skin. Jian gasped in pain when she wiped her legs down a third time, making sure no more flakes of skin slid off, leaving wide patches of her legs pink and hot.

Jian sat back and closed her eyes. The adrenaline was wearing off, leaving her exhausted. Her legs still burned, but it wasn't spreading. The ache would fade in a few days.

She breathed, slowly in, slowly out. She focused on her breath and her body. Next, she focused on the *Green Moon* and the waves that rocked against it. The water tester whirred as the halyards thrummed. Her own heartbeat echoed in her ears like a shell's cusp. Another breath in, and she let it go.

Reaching behind her, Jian found a jar of the molaluna gel she harvested. It was precious stuff; she only found the molaluna fish when its large body reflected moonlight in the dark—a silver flash in the sea. Her hands, face, and soles of her feet had been treated for many years with the gel, and it helped keep her fingers and toes whole when the current brought up the oceanox. She never possessed enough to coat her skin regularly to build up the same resistance.

Scooping out the sticky, translucent, algin-green gel, Jian rubbed it between her palms until it became warm and oily. She took a deep breath and coated her legs in the balm. The gel was immediately cooling, and Jian sighed with relief, pressing her fingers into the muscles of her calves, working out the tension that built up when the nerves in her legs were shocked by the toxisalt.

Her fingers brushed along her ankles, over the rough scars from ropes she wasn't quick enough to jump over, and then back behind her calves. There was no more gel on her hands, and while Jian knew that using more would help get rid of the last of the tingling sensation on her shins, the pot was running low. She needed to treat her face, feet, and hands at least once a week, and she was still in the oceanox current.

Sitting back against the woven plastic cushions, Jian's eyes fluttered. Exhaustion crept up on her. Spotting the tellerite delayed her final preparations, and her slip into the Tonghai drained the last of her energy. Wasn't there clean water? Would that heal her? Would that heal the world?

This was enough. Jian yawned and crawled to the lower deck, bent almost in half as she found her hammock. She angled herself in, strapping her hammock up to the ceiling to prevent her from rolling in the middle of the night. On her side, she dug into the familiar stretched-out spot where her shoulder fit perfectly.

Jian reached out for the monitor cuff. It would wake her if there was anything that needed her attention in the middle of the night. She settled down and took some kelp jerky from a small cubby above her head. She fell asleep with her mouth full and a dribble of brown paste dripping from her lips, staining the bag below her as she slept.

***

On the sixty-third day that passed without Jian seeing another person, the readings on her salinometer finally showed safe levels of oceanox. She whooped and scurried down the hatch, pulling up various bait and tackle.

Stringing up the complicated web of fishing lures typically took over an hour, but Jian's fingers were practiced and her knots were fast. She set up a series of hardbells at certain line junctions. Whenever something was hooked, a specific melody would ring out. Her father had mastered intricate trills that were bright and rushed, but all of Jian's patterns were lullabies and chants, simple and uncomplicated.

The bells weren't built for fishing days, but Jian felt guilty if they ever chimed out during her travel when the water around her was poison. It made her uneasy. They were bells of plenty and blessings and offerings. Music should be made the omen of good days.

She walked to the bow, playfully plucking the lines as she stepped over them, catching them with the tips of her toes, her boat resonant. The waves that her hull dove through added to the symphony. She sat at the bow of her boat and looked forward. Jian took a deep breath, held it, and let it out as her bow nosed down into the water.

Some of the spray hit her face, her cheeks and neck. She kept her eyes closed and breathed in as the *Green Moon* rose on the crest of another wave, the bright sunlight hitting her solarails and reflecting warm golds down on her nose. The *Moon's* bow nosed down again, water flew up, hitting her hands and knees, and she smiled.

She breathed in with the waves and out with the Tonghai. Her lungs the wind, her blood the current. Wasn't her blood metallic like the nox? Didn't she cry sludge-salt tears? There was no proof other than her own body that told her that the world deserved to be Tonghai, that her small boat and small struggles were part of a larger current, a larger weather pattern. There was something shifting in the skies, Jian knew it. She was that shift, in every breath in every tack. Jian was the prayer alive.

The first bell that rang out, crystalline and bright, held nothing but red kelp. Using a small screener she tested the kelp periodically as she hauled it on board, but all indicators read safe to handle. As Jian pulled it under the lifelines, she picked off small ten-legged crablings, throwing them into a cone-shaped bucket. She was fast, flicking them with deadly accuracy into the pot, the mushy knocks of shell against plasticine creating an odd rhythm to accompany her chimes.

She hung the kelp out to cure under the solarsails with U-shaped needles, securing them to the wires underneath the booms. Halfway through the task, another chime rang out.

Jian carefully picked her way over the lines toward the sibilant bell. She tugged on the line gently, testing the resistance on it. Taut, and growing harder. Jian found some slack and wrapped the line around a horn, activating the pressure gauge. She strapped into a trap harness and stepped outside of the lifeline, leaning out over the Tonghai. Using her body as leverage, Jian pressed down on the fishing line to give it more leeway, and when she lifted herself up, the horn turned to pull in the slack.

Slowly, in inches, Jian measured her body against the strength of whatever creature she caught on her line. The hooked beast was heavy, and it was trying to swim away, not down. It wasn't the panicked motion of the smaller, more mindless fish, but a controlled, invested focus of a beast intent on getting away. There was a long way to go, and no way to see what was on the line. Taking a deep breath, Jian leveraged her body up and then pushed back down again.

The sun beat on her back and shoulders. She dripped sweat back into the Tonghai, an offering of salt to salt.

Jian had only a concept of prayer, only knew parts and portions and half the theory tied to prayer. Her father taught her chants that turned into many hums and murmurs meant for repetition with intentions and motivations, but right now, her only goal was on the other end of a plastigut line, and her only focus was on the dark water underneath her.

Jian prayed to the water; to stay clean and feed her. She prayed to the spinning horn on her boat to keep turning. Jian took a deep breath and prayed to the wind to keep her sails full. Jian let her breath turn the ocean's prayer wheel, each movement of her body against the water an effort for the dharma within the warm, clean current. She moved the wheels of absolution as a fish moves in the ocean.

It was night when Jian finally hauled the creature near enough to see it. When she saw the sloped ridge line breaking the water, she hoped it was an eel or another long, ray-finned beast. It would be easy to chop up and haul into the boat piece by piece. In a stroke of luck, the creature swam toward the boat, and the horn spun in the slack. Jian's smile faded fast as the lumins under the water exposed its full size and shape.

A turtle. A massive, fully-grown, algin-green turtle.

Jian's arms shook from exhaustion and disappointment as the turtle swam up to her hull. She slumped onto the boat, watching as all her prayers turned back on her.

She couldn't bring the turtle into the boat. She couldn't. The *Green Moon* was small, with no crane. There was no second boat to help her net the turtle and drag it up the transom. A day of work all spent bringing in a beast that she could take nothing from. Jian sat down on the deck. The turtle swam over and knocked its head against the hull. The edge of its flipper slid under the boat, knocking against the rudder, and the boat shifted.

"Stop that." Her voice was hoarse and dry.

The turtle knocked against the rudder again.

Jian shifted forward, sliding her legs off the side of the boat. The back of the hull sloped together and down, and the area near the stern was lower to the water. The turtle was large enough that her taped-up feet could touch the top of its leathery dome.

Her toes dug into the algin that grew across the turtle like a long beard, trailing behind it at least three feet. She swallowed and closed her eyes, overwhelmed suddenly, tearing up. Sliding in between the top and middle lifelines, Jian curled over herself, setting her feet firmly against the turtle's back. She sucked in a breath and wrapped her arms tightly across her torso.

With her feet on the turtle's shell, Jian sobbed. The whole day spent bringing in a creature too big for her to handle, too old for her to understand, too strong to give up. Her tears were so dry they left gritty streaks under her eyes.

Underneath her toes, the turtle swam next to the boat.

The sunsails whirring to life in the morning light woke her. She had fallen asleep, rocked by the *Moon* and secured in her trap harness, too exhausted to move.

She looked down and was startled to see the turtle looking up at her. It swam placidly next to the boat, not pulling against the plastigut. Its large fins—each easily the full length of one of Jian's arms—waved gently.

The shame was immediate. Here was a living creature dragged like a downed flag in the water. She tried to stand too fast and her legs almost collapsed. Jian gripped the lifeline tightly and took a slow, deep breath. She focused; she was here, with the turtle and the Tonghai.

"I am sorry," Jian said to the turtle, walking over to the horn. There wouldn't be any way to get the hook back, and maybe that was enough of a loss to make up for the way she treated the beast. She crouched by the rotating horn, taking her knife out of its pouch.

The blade stopped an inch from the line. She swallowed and looked down at the turtle.

Its head, large, scarred, was turned towards her, beak open. Jian saw it, deeply. Saw how it survived, saw that it swam fast and strong, that it understood more than Jian understood. Jian hesitated to let it go. What other beast would know her as this turtle knew her?

The turtle blinked, the murky third eyelid pulling back to reveal the true sheen of its eyes. Its eye, dark blue, dappled with golden flecks, stared at her.

Constellations turned within the turtle's eye, stars brightly shining and spinning. Jian's loneliness ran through like a shock of lightning. She pulled the knife up and the turtle was free.

The turtle continued to swim next to the boat, now without a tether, and for a few seconds Jian allowed herself to believe that the creature would stay with her. Then the turtle blinked, and the stars in its eye disappeared, and the spell was broken. It ducked its head and dove under the water, sliding into the depth of the Tonghai where Jian could not follow.

She watched the space on the ocean where she last saw the turtle until her eyes hurt. She blinked, and the reflection of the waves left something wrong on her memory. She was lost at sea, and wondered if the feeling of the algin in-between her toes was enough to convince her that the turtle was ever there at all.

***

Not long after Jian set the turtle free, she spotted sails on the horizon. Quickly, Jian readied for trade. She set her tiller and charted a course diverting north, towards the second boat. There was little fear of pirates on the Tonghai. There was too much risk for both parties. Kill or be killed meant that everyone died. Instead of turning away, Jian pulled her sails closer to the center line as she went tighter to the wind. She found her radio and tested it, pleased that crud hadn't built up on the mastennae.

"Hailing the schooner with blue sails, this is Jian-" Her voice cracked, and she leaned over to grab a skein of water for her parched throat. There was a soft crack on the other end of the radio and Jian took a deep breath.

"This is Jian of the *Green Moon*. I have turned up to you."

She paused, waiting. A hiss of static, then nothing. Another longer hiss. Jian felt her nerves in her throat. She glanced at the kelp dots painted on the inside of the hull. The boat rode on the waves gently as Jian took a long breath, closing her eyes.

"This is Jian of the *Green Moon*. I have trade and..."

She trailed off, her mouth dry. Another burst of static.

This time, she listened. A pattern. She found a kelp-charcoal pencil and wrote out static and pause as it came across the radio.

"*Head up. Have trade. Return happy. Head up. Have trade.*"

Jian bit her tongue to keep from grinning like a fool. She opened up the line again.

"Thank you Blue Sail. I am heading up. I have fish, some spare tech. I can repair solarsails," she said, her voice breaking again. She glanced out at the other boat, and listened. Over the radio came another series of silence and static; "*We are* Waka Manawa Ora. *Hail* Green Moon."

When Jian came close enough to the *Ora*, she saw that it comprised of three hulls, the smaller outriggers on either side each as long as the *Green Moon*. The middle hull, the largest and longest, stuck out another twenty feet, with at least two levels into the hull. It was very impressive, and Jian sailed up slowly, reefing her sails to control her approach.

There were five people lined up against the safeties. Jian held up one hand as she maneuvered the *Moon* with the other. The hull of her boat knocked against the starboard outrigger as she docked.

Jian swallowed, took a deep breath, spoke in commonate: "Hail."

A wiry woman with long hair, braided back, stepped towards Jian and bowed, holding her hand out. Along the *Ora's* hull, the rest of the group hooked the *Moon's* lines to raft their boats together. Jian smiled brightly at the crew, and looked up at the woman, taking her hand.

Jian was pulled onto the *Ora* easily—the woman's broad shoulders flexed as Jian's feet landed on the rosin-coated deck. She pulled Jian into a hug, holding her tightly. Jian let a breath out, and wrapped her arms around the darker woman, closing her eyes. She felt strong, sun-warmed, and whole. She felt something rise up, and almost began to cry, simple human touch nearly enough to unspool Jian.

"Welcome, friend," the woman murmured, taking a step back. "You honor us."

Jian nodded, bowing back. "You honor me," her voice was soft and gravelly.

The woman nodded, gesturing. "Eat with us. We have plenty on this clean rise."

Jian swallowed and looked around the large boat. The *Ora* was deeper than she thought, and could probably house fifteen comfortably. How they survived on the Tonghai—a clan floating among the poison—was remarkable. It made her eyes tear up, the resilience of people. She took a deep breath.

"You honor me," she repeated as the woman led her across the netting to the center hull, and into the depths of the *Ora*.

***

The meal was roasted fish, a salad with spicy peppers that the gardener, Yerva, grew from a mix of kelp-soil, excrement, and ground-up fishbones. Jian's mouth burned at the spice, but she picked out the orange-red disks and popped them in her mouth, crunching down. Boolie quickly offered her water, holding her up as she coughed.

The laughter around her as her eyes prickled and her face became warm made her cry, but she was able to blame it on the pepper. She turned, could smell the sweetness of Boolie's skin, the heat that radiated off her even in the cool evening.

After dinner, Boolie, offered to escort her back to the *Moon* for the night, keeping a steadying hand on Jian's back.

"We will trade tomorrow," Boolie said, looking at the stars tattooed along Jian's arms. "We have a sheet of solar for you to look over." Jian blinked and nodded, not moving away from Boolie, watching her with clear eyes.

"Thank you."

Jian stood at the edge of the *Ora*, looking over Boolie. The captain caught Jian's eye, and Jian flushed red again, but this time without any spice to blame. Boolie caught her jaw next, and kissed her gently.

Jian was not so gentle, pulling Boolie onto the *Moon*, and taking her belowdecks, tangling her hands in Boolie's long hair.

***

In the pre-dawn shine of the morning, Jian instructed the youngest onboard the *Ora*—a small, green-eyed boy named Té—on how to properly lay out the solarsails. Té ran around, pulling on the tack to tighten the sail. All three sides of this sail—the leech, luff, and foot—had to be without creases or Jian wouldn't be able to properly see the connections. Once Té lashed the tack to a horn on the far outrigger, Jian began the painstaking process of testing the connections and reflecthread woven throughout the teflon sails.

"Will it all glow again?" Té asked, standing at Jian's right, holding her bag of tools tightly. "It should," Jian said softly. She inspected the reflecthread and the hex-panel it was woven into, then

moved down, hands running over the edge of the sail. Fraying at the borders was the most common, but the easiest to fix. She spotted the first short thread about a third of the way down the sail and gestured for Té to sit down next to her on the netting.

"See this?" Jian held up the edge, showing him the broken connection.

Té nodded. Jian quickly took a bit of wiring and a bit of tack from the bag Té held open and rubbed the thread until it became smooth. Then, she laid the wire down to the border and covered it with the tack again. She applied a sealant made from the intestinal lining of the alloshark, and then leaned over to blow on it. Té watched with wide eyes.

She finished mending the connection and scooted down the net. The solarsail had to be up the mast and boom to absorb and provide energy to the boat, so most of the work Jian was doing wouldn't be seen until they tested the sail out in the light. It was tedious work, and Jian could see that Té's attention was fading as he glanced over his shoulder, his hands going from his knees to his face to the sail.

"I can take the bag now," she said, holding her hand out. "Go play somewhere else."

The child wavered for a second, and Jian smiled at him.

"Thank you for your work today."

Té nodded, pulled the bag off his belt, and handed it over. He ran across the boat and strapped into the security lines, called for another member of the crew—his mother, presumably—to check his harness. The instant he was approved, Té scrambled under the boat, setting up fishing lines and lures attached to the side of the outrigger. Jian wondered if she could set up a similar rig on her boat.

Lost in thought for a few minutes, Jian didn't notice Boolie until the woman knelt down next to her.

"How does she look?"

Jian shrugged, smiling at her hands. "Not bad. None of the previous repairs have been damaged."

"Good to hear. We ran out of sealant a few months ago and never found a suitable material replacement."

Jian nodded. "I sailed over a pod of shark five weeks ago. Was able to get some small ones on board."

"I'm grateful for it."

"So am I."

Jian nudged Boolie's leg, and the captain slid down the net, giving Jian room to follow. They were silent down the leech and the foot of the sails. Jian inspecting, fixing, nudging. Boolie smiling, touching her arm, asking about each star written there.

"I'm headed west," Jian said finally, after they had clambered around the entire sail.

"We're chasing the warm current," Boolie responded, looking over at the other end of the boat where Té and Yerva were pulling up a small octopus. "We'll be heading northward soon."

Jian nodded, keeping her head down, smiling. She was so pleased that Boolie was near her, and as she worked, she occasionally reached over, touching Boolie's hands.

Boolie was about to say something when a strange noise cut through the bustle of activity on the boat.

Rustling, then, a sharp caw.

"Birds!" Boolie yelled and jumped up. She quickly ran to the center hull, joined by two more of her crew. They started scaling the masts as Jian watched, eyes wide.

"Bearing down!" The navigator—a stout man name Harral—called out. Boolie responded with a sharp whistle, gesturing south. Turning towards the port side, across the bow of her own *Moon* (still lashed to the *Ora's* outrigger), Jian saw the flock, a feathered cyclone of birds that drifted up in expanding helixine patterns. Such creatures were rare, and Jian quickly waved for Té to come over and help her flake the sail for storage.

The *Ora* turned around and approached the birds from leeward, giving them more control over their speed. The sail safely belowdecks, Jian found a vantage point on the starboard outrigger. The birds cycloned upward slowly. They had long wings, tilted down into the center of the vortex. The tips of their wings were curled upwards, and Jian's father used to tell her that this adaption helped create a vacuum to draw the flock upwards, allowing the entire group to fly for weeks at a time without touching the water.

At the center of their vortex, where the flock dropped down into the sea, was a large floating mass. It was bright green, with shimmering red stripes up its sides.

She called Té over, pointing at the colorful creature.

"That is a nesting nomad," Jian said, her eyes on the bowl of its center. "There will be bird's eggs in the middle. They are protecting it."

"We'll take the eggs?" Té asked.

Jian shrugged, looking up at the members of the crew. They were all setting up small hand-harpoons. "We take the birds for flesh and feathers. We leave the eggs for more birds."

Té nodded, settling down next to Jian. The *Ora* slowed down, almost crawling as they came within throwing distance. Boolie gave another series of whistles, and hand-barbs flew from the boat, spearing birds' wings. They dragged the birds into the boat like kites, dropping them down to Yerva, who snapped their necks and laid them out carefully, placing them over a channeled part of the hull that collected any blood that dripped off them.

Jian was silent, noting the cruel efficiency of the harpooning. After almost two dozen of the creatures were brought on board Boolie let out another sharp whistle and called for a halt.

The rest of the day was spent plucking the oil-slick feathers, setting aside the offal to cure in brine as a bait reserve, and butchering birds. Dinner that night was birds over fresh seaweed, and Jian licked the meat juices from her fingers as Boolie's hip pressed against hers.

On the *Moon*, Jian dozed on the couch, curled against Boolie's larger frame, listening to the dual patterns of the waves and Boolie's breathing. She sighed, pressed her face against Boolie's neck, and fell into a deep sleep, smelling birdflesh on her breath.

***

The next morning, after Jian tested the *Ora's* solarsail and felt its heat, she prepared to leave. The *Moon* was now stocked with octopus and birds, in addition to the tackle and thread given for the sail repair. She stood on the bow, testing the stays, and then wandered back over to the starboard side of the boat, looking up at the members of the *Ora* who were lining up to say farewell.

The woman who minded Té apologized, and said he was too sad to say goodbye. Harral gave her a needle's point from a compass on a small chain, and fastened it around her neck. Yerva gave her a bowl of bone-soil that was already sprouting up a few seedlings.

"Peppers," she muttered, giving her a hug. "Careful harvesting them—they will burn your hands."

When Boolie embraced her, Jian wanted to cut the *Moon* free and bind herself to the *Ora* forever. It was the pang of an oncoming loneliness. Boolie kissed her temple and pulled away. Jian forced herself to take a step back, and then step over the *Ora's* lifelines, down to the deck of the *Green Moon*.

Harrel cast off her bow, and Boolie the stern, and Jian cradled the bowl as her raised sails caught the wind and spun her down, pulling her away from the comfort of company. She raised a hand as she drifted, and then began to sail away.

"Hail, *Waka Manawa Ora*, fair winds." Jian convinced herself her voice didn't crack. Boolie raised a hand in response, but her voice was snatched by a gust that dropped from the clouds, pulling the lighter *Green Moon* away from the trimaran.

The *Ora* sailed, and Jian kept her eyes fixed on the boat until she could not see the figures on the sides, until the sails were just blue glimmers that disappeared on the Tonghai's horizon. Jian sat in the cockpit, cradling the seedling bowl, trying not to think of the folly of chasing the stars to the west, following the patterns on her arms that grew closer the sky.

She spent her life searching for Tiger King, for the Escapement-sky. She desperately pursued the season and the hemisphere that would show the asterisms on her hands. She would not be pulled off course for the sake of a week of companionship. There was weak water, the floating river, and it was clean and it would take her to the sea of sweet fish.

Night fell, and Jian looked up at the garbage ring that crossed the sky. The moon was half-gone and Jian was alone on her small ship, with only dead birds and pepper sprouts for company.

***

The first morning Jian woke without Boolie next to her, without the *Ora* knocking against kelp-macramed buoys, she placed the first small algin dot on the plastifiber hull of her boat.

It wouldn't help her to dwell on that lonely dot, and she quickly made her way to the deck. Jian checked the sails and her heading, and then spun the salinometer. The oceanox levels remained in the safe zone, the cool clean water still too heavy for the warmer poison it rise to the surface. The current would shift soon; it's why the *Ora* went north toward the cold water.

Jian decided not to set up the full symphony of strings and bells, and settled for a half-chorus of tack rigged only from the transom of the boat. There were hours of work to do repairing netting, and she started by stripping the leafy parts of kelpweed from its stalk. The weaving required concentration and swift fingers, and Jian crouched over the work, focused. No bells rang out, and time passed, the pooling of netting spreading like a leaky bilge around her feet.

The sun was high when Jian finally sat up straight, cracked her back, and looked around, blinking. The bells were soft, but no chime indicated a catch. The sound helped lull her into her craft. She stood, hands on her lower back and stretched, closing her eyes as she turned her face upwards. What kind of prayers come from knotwork, Jian wondered. What constellations turned underneath her hands?

She hummed and turned toward the bow. The solarsails were up, glowing bright and creating a circuit of warmth across her boat. Stepping up on the cockpit seat, Jian walked along the *Moon's* deck. As her eyes adjusted to the reflection off the Tonghai she froze. Her hand tightened around the maststay, and she took a deep breath.

On the horizon, tall, stalk-like orange protrusions jutted out of the water. Dozens of them, orange and white, with silver streaks emanating from the tip down to the base, hidden under the water. Jian's mouth was dry. She had no idea what these were.

They undulated gently on the horizon, the silver along their sides flashing as the protrusions waved.

Jian knew that she should bear down, pick up speed downwind and avoid this new mystery that rose from the depths. That was the right decision, the good decision, and she knew deep in her bones that this was not something she understood.

It was not the decision she made. She scrambled back to the cockpit, bringing in the *Moon's* sails, heading up to the distant creatures.

They were cerata. Horns on the horizon.

There was one grouping, and then a second, and she got closer and realized there was a third, all shimmering gently, sunset-colored, reflecting across each other. The cerata were moving in a circle, around each other. It wasn't obvious until she got closer that these massive, soft-skinned beasts were swimming together. Jian had never seen giant nudibranch before, she had never even considered that they were real—how did they survive the oceanox? Jian could see through their skin to the soft cartilage-like tissue that went through the cerata.

She could hardly think straight as she sailed closer, her hand tight on the tiller. The cerata towered above her mast, the giants not even considering the *Green Moon* as they swam. Not in circles, but in a strange interwoven pattern, one that mimicked the netting Jian tied together for hours. Jian wanted to cry again, the same feeling when she saw the asterisms in the turtle's eye. Every creature overwhelmed her, made her feel desperately connected to the world around her. Giants still searched the ocean, the Tonghai could sustain beasts, of course it could sustain her. She turned a dial on the tiller, and the forward pumps turned on, pushing from the bow, stopping the boat, still fully-rigged, from moving forward.

She stood then, knowing she should turn away, knowing that this was foolish, and fools did not last on the Tonghai, knowing this and standing anyway, she walked to the bow. She slid around the forestay, onto the pulpit. She slid out over the water, her toes curled around the mesh grid. Jian took a deep breath and reached out towards one of the undulating cerata, stretching with her full body and her fingers, the bright colors hypnotizing.

Overhead, a tellerite spun. Jian looked up, eyes huge, the craft lower in the sky than she had ever seen any of the strange vehicles fly. It was V-shaped, the point moving forward, the two terminals of the shape rotating, the stems emitting a white power source that kept the tellerite going. Jian was so distracted by the tellerite that when the nudibranch came closer, a massive cerata knocking against the *Green Moon* Jian's whole body went into the water, and she fell head-first into the Tonghai.

The massive bodies of the nudibranchs created a current that swept her under their bellies, the cerata and plumes on their sides pushing water down, and Jian along with it. She couldn't swim against the beasts, and tried to dive deeper to get away from their pull, but the vacuum sucked her into the center of the circling creatures. They pulled her in.

Jian struggled and couldn't swim back to the *Moon*. Like a whirlpool, she was sucked into the eye of it. Turned around, she fought to reach the surface—any surface. She grabbed onto a cerata, but it was too soft, and she found no grip. The bright lights of the horns were blurring together, and the brightness of the beasts did nothing to guide her. Jian's air was running out—the pressure on her chest more painful than any fall or hurt. She took one last furious kick towards a bright flash of light, and broke the surface.

Her eyes were wide as she gasped for air, treading water.

It was night-time. She looked around quickly, still gasping, her adrenaline pumping in her ears. It had been day when she fell. She swallowed, looked up, and saw the V-shaped tellerite still nearby, moving slowly across the sky. A bit ahead of the teller-ite bobbed the *Green Moon*, still locked in the holding position where she left it.

Jian almost sunk back under the Tonghai. Her arms hurt. They ached from her wrists to her shoulders. She turned on her back, took a deep breath, and then began to swim to her boat.

It took nearly ten minutes for her to get to the hull, and she rested against the transom, holding onto the pull-down ladder. Jian looked up, blinking salt water out of her eyes. The tellerite was still moving, but now even slower. It turned slightly, as if search-ing for the right star to anchor on.

Jian swallowed and heaved herself into the *Moon*. She sat heav-ily in the cockpit, her whole body sagging. The tellerite was still there, hanging, moving slowly.

The craft ducked down, and then, like a finger drawing the con-stellations between stars, it moved in a set pattern, nosing into the Tonghai. Jian could be imagining things, delirious after fall-ing into the water. She forced herself up, holding onto the life-lines as she walked along the deck. She sat down heavily, eyes fixed on the tellerite.

As the V of the craft lifted out of the Tonghai, a waterfall streamed down from its bow. Jian's pushed at her eyes until they watered, but the water continued to pour. Her mouth was dry as the spacecraft spun towards her, the ends of the V's submerging themselves into the water, the apex of the craft slowly turning to point up.

The water continued to flow from the apex, not down to the bubbling, white-silver waves, but up into the heavens, a river of water ascending into the sky.

Jian's breath caught in her throat.

She ran back to the cockpit, her hands fumbling with the dial on the tiller. The pumps at the bow stopped, and the *Green Moon*, running on stored sols, shot forward. She aimed the bow in the middle of the two stems, her eyes huge as the *Moon* sailed in between the engines. She looked up, at the river that streamed up from the apex of the tellerite, and nudged her boat forward, up onto the waterfall, and then onto the weak river. Tears began to slide down her face as she rose above the Tonghai, sailing on the sky's clean water.

Don't Stop

Reneé Bibby

Reneé Bibby is the director of The
Writers Studio Tucson, where she
teaches advanced and beginner creative
writing workshops. Her work has
appeared in PRISM International, Thin
Air, Third Point Press, The Worcester
Review, and Wildness. Her stories have
been nominated for Pushcart Prizes and
Best Small Fictions.

Keesha craves the soothing that comes with nighttime driving. The road's yellow line threading luxuriously, slowly, in the highbeams of the truck, hypnotizing her into a nighttime fugue of not thinking, but not sleeping—an in-between state as mild and sweet as twilight.It's her fourth day into a 2,000-mile trek across Alaska, four hours into darkness, and she isn't soothed. She is stabbed awake by thoughts of home.

Stabbed by the memories of the most adrenaline-spiked moments: the curb at the front of the hospital jarring her little Nissan Sentra sideways as she squealed cockeyed into a no-parking zone; the blue swish of parting doors and the face of the front-desk woman shuttering closed at her sister's name; the stiff back of the head nurse leading her through a warren of white rooms to her niece, Dahlia.

Stabbed by the memory of Dahlia, swaddled in white, except for a pink blanket pressed to her snot-crusted, spit-streaked face speckled red from the implosion of windshield glass. White butterfly Band-Aids criss crossed her face. *Hey, kid,* Keesha signed. Of all the things she could have said in that dismal hour, and she sees it on repeat, again and again—her own hands doing that stupidly cheery sign, *hey, kid.*

A memory like a horse-kick to her chest, when Dahlia looked away.

A glimpse of her sister, a white sheet covering everything except a spread of dark hair—

But then—at the very edge of the rig's high-beams, a movement—and the next second a blown-out white shape on the yellow line of the road; a mirror flash of eyes; a tall, human shaped figure.

Keesha brakes, pure instinct, hauls the wheel right, even if impact wasn't imminent, the high-beams giving her the benefit of distance. The truck slides to a stop in the gravel of the shoulder, half-up an incline, headlights beaming toward the Kenai Mountains.

With only two hours of service left on her seventy, enough to reach Seward and unload her payload, she should kick the truck into gear and keep going. A delay would force dispatch to reroute someone else to unload. She's managed her time pristinely; she knows every route, every refuel, every unload to the minute and it's been years since she missed the payout of unloading. If she doesn't look back, she can tell herself it was a moose or an elk. Native, natural, and no reason to investigate. *But what if it wasn't an animal?* The pale silhouette of a person cuts the blue-black square of darkness in her side mirror.

Keesha clicks the cabin door open, and the greedy cold sucks her breath away. She hops down to bundle up: a jacket, windbreaker, gloves, a scarf wound around her neck and over her mouth. She slides her phone into her back pocket and the pepper spray from under her seat into her coat pocket.

When she squints, she confirms it wasn't an illusion, a person-shaped glare of moonlight, standing right on the yellow line of the road. Without venturing closer, Keesha calls, "Hullo?" The person doesn't turn.

She walks seven or so paces. Stops. The paleness isn't a matter of winter clothes, the unadorned head not a fuzzy white hat. A naked woman. The spine knobbed and shadowed, thin arms widen at the elbows, the butt flat, curved low by the decline of advanced age.

"Ma'am!" Keesha jogs around the woman.

She is moonbeam pure; her arms hang at her sides, and her mouth is slack and wide. Her eyes, dark and shadowed by long lashes, swivel to Keesha. A tongue moves to touch top teeth. Keesha steps back, an avoidance and retreat as instinctual as braking, but from what she cannot say. After all, it's a naked 80-something-year-old woman who needs help. The woman must belong to someone; a daughter or a nurse's aide will come back into a room to find it empty, discarded bedclothes just outside the pool of porch light. A frantic call to the police.

Cold feels like a drill, sharp and boring between the cracks of jacket and jean and sock. The woman's skin is crisped white, nubbed with goose bumps. Her bare feet flat against the dark asphalt, as if she were at the beach, defy comprehension—there had to be a medical explanation, diabetic neuropathy or vascular disease.

Keesha crimps the scarf against her mouth, releasing a small enough space to say, "Ma'am, can I help you?'

Keesha thinks of a praying mantis as the woman tilts her head and takes a step back, then another.

"Hey, hey," Keesha croons, "it's okay."

Now perched at the edge of the road, an arm behind her and her back foot poised, the woman is still as a tree. It's so quiet, the air seems to absorb sound as if the atmosphere wishes to obscure them, yet the moon is bright enough to enflame the clouds between and illuminate the white fluff of the woman's hair, the length of her arms, the small sparse triangle of pubic hair.

"I won't hurt you," Keesha reassures her. "How about I call someone, yeah?"

Keesha slips her phone out, ready, squinting against the blaze of the phone's cheery lights. She is blinded, but she senses the woman move. Keesha follows her off the road, nearly losing her in the thick thrum of dark trees and bushes. "Hey, no, wait, I'm putting away my phone."

Crouched, arched like a cat, the woman swivels slowly to face Keesha, unbothered by the branches plucking her hair into a halo, the dark leaves shadowing her face. If Keesha unfocuses her vision, assesses from the side of her eyes instead of searching, the woman fuzzes into nothingness. She could be dappling of light in the brush.

Keesha debates. This isn't just a matter of lifting a brittle old lady into the truck. It will take effort to coax the disoriented woman into safety. In training, then again in orientation, and later as an occasional reminder from dispatch, the directive is: "Don't stop." Stopping messes up your OTR; helping opens you up to lawsuits. A stopped truck is a beacon for theft and attacks. That edict usually absolved her—made it easy to blow by broken-down motorists and hitchhikers. The number and manner of half-crushed, wild creatures she's swerved around in the road, much less the birds and rabbits she's pulled from her truck's grille—a taxidermist phantasmagoria that's never given her a night of unrest.

Unbidden, Keesha remembers a chocolate lab off I-10, whuffling along the shoulder, oblivious to roaring trucks and cars. He wasn't a lean, angry creature to be sheared off by the natural selection of the road; his tail-wagging, barrel-bodied gait and green collar were the pure, stupid charm of a pet. Keesha saw him a mile ahead and thought *I should stop, because someone loves him,* but below that conscious thought ran the constant clicking calculation of distance, rates, pay and time, which spit out a ticker tape showing hours left to drive to Houston. As quick as that, the urge to help was overturned, *don't have the time; I'm sure he'll be fine.* She blew by him waddling along in a straight line, but in her side mirror she saw him dart left into traffic. A screech of brake and a Ford F-150 knocked him clear across the road.

Now, in the deep darkness and cold of the night, she remembers him pinwheeling in the gray haze of the Houston air. The hot squeeze of guilt overwhelms every sliver of disquiet. She reassures the woman: "I won't call anybody. I put the phone away, see? How about you tell me your name?"

The muscles of the woman's neck tighten, a sideways glance and narrowed eyes, and finally, words: "Where's the shimmer?"

A shiver shoots through Keesha at the sound—flat, without any inflection, but with a strange under-pitch, a reverberation of the words, slightly out of sync and warped lower like the bending, fraying ribbons of northern lights vibrating above them.

There's something not right here, but she can't say what, an ineffable unsettling she would never be able to explain to authorities in the shining normality of daylight, and if she leaves it has to be for a reason so solid, she can look someone in the eye later and explain exactly why she abandoned their grandmother.

Keesha suggests, "The northern lights, yeah? The shimmer? They're above us, see?"

The woman tilts her head back, exposing the corded tension of her neck, and regards the sky.

"Yeah, see? You've found the shimmer...Want to watch from my truck? It's nice and warm inside my truck." Reassured by a quick touch to the pepper spray in her right pocket, Keesha inventories the rest of her pockets' contents: a wad of Kleenex, a snarl of bobby pins, sprigs of hair, an over-stretched hair band, a Lego person, dollar and change, and a half-eaten bag of gummi bears in her parka. Was it just a few day ago that she'd cracked the bag open to shovel a handful into Dahlia's hands and quiet her signing, *Auntie, where are you going? When will you be back?* Providence has transmuted that anguish into luck. "Want a gummi?"

The bag crinkling open is a firework in the quiet. Keesha mimes putting one into her mouth and extends her arm to the fullest.

Keesha blinks and the woman is there, head angled, to inspect the contents of the bag with one eye. She plucks a handful and stuffs it in her mouth. Keesha is treated to the slicing of gummi bear by oddly angled teeth. Bits of bear slop outside the rim of her mouth, opening and closing wider and darker than seems necessary for such simple food. A dark tongue roots along the edges of lips, worming around for strays as if hunting on its own volition. The woman hums.

"You liked that, yeah? Come on, have some more." Keesha takes a few steps back, frost crackling under her boots, as she leads the woman to the road. The woman darts forward for another handful of gummies. More smacking of lips, slurping, and a low, constant hum. She even closes her eyes, following the packet of food unerringly as if she can smell the gummies.

They progress across the road to her rig.

Keesha sights the truck over her shoulder, but with gummies almost gone and the woman so focused on the food in her hand, she can't sort what trick will get the woman into the safety of her cabin if they run out. Being out of tricks seems to be this year's theme. Faced with a mourning and listless Dahlia, Keesha had caved on junk food every evening. She'd kicked the challenge to her neighbor Lorena, who agreed to watch Dahlia this time because Keesha promised to be back by Thursday. "Maybe see if you can get her to eat regular food. Give her some fruit, yeah?" Dahlia had looked up, tuning into something the women were saying, and signed, "*banana?*" Lorena didn't know sign language, so Keesha translated, "maybe a banana."

Keesha remembers what else she has now. "Oh, dang, looks like the gummies are all gone. Did you want a banana?"

At the truck door, the woman licks her finger, quickly, noisily then drops her arms as if she's lost control over them. Nothing changes on the woman's face. No indication of having heard.

Keesha makes the sign for banana. Reaching behind without taking her eyes off the woman, Keesha clicks open the cabin of her truck and gestures inside like a hostess welcoming someone to a party. As soon as it opens, the woman climbs up in a smooth, swift ascent, limber and strong. Keesha uses the handles to haul herself up to usher the woman across the bench-seat to the passenger side.

In the buttery cabin light, the woman watches Keesha unzip, peel off gloves, rub her hands together, unwind the scarf, and swipe a tissue over the drip of her nose. Keesha asks, "aren't you cold, ma'am?"

The keys rattle as Keesha slides them into the ignition, but the woman's head comes up quick, a hand on the door handle, poised to open it. This old woman, knobbed and thinned to mere skin droopy as soft cheese would do it, too—crack the door open and skitter into the darkness, across the highway, and into the wilds around Bear Lake faster than Keesha could possibly chase her. Keesha releases the key, hands up in surrender.

"Okay, I won't start the truck. How about that banana?" She roots around in the plastic bag from the Circle K for an anemic banana, bruised brown—all that is left from a lunch of a pre-packaged ham sandwich, Cheetos, and an Arizona Iced Tea. She peels the banana and passes it over.

The woman crams all of it in her mouth at once, blowing out her cheeks and pressing two hands to her lips to keep any from spilling. Her jaw flexes, her breath huffs loud in the cabin as she chews with schlocking and slurping.

The cabin is sweet with the scent of banana, barely covering the pungency of the unwashed woman, an intense mixture of sour sweat, urine, and metallics—iron minerals and mica. Dark scabs and fresh red welts crisscross her forearms and thighs, the teeth mark of brambles and other sharp flora of the underbrush.

"How long you been out there, lady?" Keesha murmurs, watching the sinew and tendons of her throat force down a lump of banana, not expecting an answer.

"Since the dark." In the cabin, her voice sounds normal, not like before, and not frail like an old woman's, but firm—powerful enough to get around the banana.

"Dark? Just tonight? That can't be right."

The woman chews slowly, pausing to pump chunks of food down. The jut of the woman's brow shadows her eyes, but the planes of her face are sere, stark white in the light of the cab. Keesha can't tell what's off, what small proportion of composition is misaligned to make the woman's face seem so long, the outward swell of mouth like mandibles.

Keesha touches the spray in her pocket.

"It shimmers." The woman is nearly done with the banana.

"Yeah, you said that earlier...You mean the northern lights, right?"

"It shimmers, and They come."

"They?"

The woman shakes her head a few times, taps her hands on her forehead as if she's trying to shake loose a thought. She whimpers and suddenly leans forward to peer through the windshield, tilting her head up, left, then right to scan the clouded expanse of sky and whispers, "Yes."

Keesha's stomach sours. *Oh shit, you picked up a crazy woman.* Why had she ignored the rule? Don't stop. Don't pick people up.

Leaning now into the light of the cabin, the woman's eyes swivel to look at her.

She should just let the woman go. Release her like a spider caught in a cup—not even waiting until the sun comes up—let her creep back into the cold wilds. She's about to suggest it, a mutual parting of ways, but then the woman jerks upright and reaches across Keesha to unhook the CB microphone. She clears her throat into the chatter channel, knocking Keesha's knee with a hand as she twirls the tuning dial. Her fingers are exceptionally long and thin, almost bone-colored in the gloom of the truck. She dials past stations, crackling static followed by bursts of human voices, to stop at a frequency that is quiet, but not empty—a hum that veers briefly into the strata of static. Keesha's teeth ache, she rubs her jaw, tugs at her ear lobes to ease the tension of the sound, a subsonic ratcheting of insect wings vibrating through the bones of her face.

Pressing the call button down hard, the woman holds the mic like she's done it before, hovering it close to her lips. She closes her eyes, tilts her head, and presses it to her throat, hard enough to dent the skin, pushing it around along the threads of tendons until stopping high up under the chin. Keesha's lips have been against that mic, it has her spittle, her atoms on it, and the sight of it nestled against the woman's throat is unbearably intimate. Keesha wants to jerk it free by the cord.

"That's not how you talk on it."

She said the same thing nearly six months ago to Dahlia, with an entirely different tone. Her sister, Jazmine, and Dahlia made a short car trip to Bellevue to meet her at the weigh station with a picnic lunch. Soon as she was in the cab, Jazmine placed a spiny succulent on Keesha's dash, reflexively signing as she spoke, "I brought you a cute succulent. *Aloinopsis luckhoffii*." She even finger-spelled the plant name.

"No."

"Come on, Keesh. I did research on what could work. It needs, like, no water; it'll be hard to kill it."

"It's going to cook on my dash, like all the others. I've already told you this: I drive through cold parts of the world, but the dash is a convection oven. I don't want to watch it slowly die."

"Fine." Jazmine rubbed her fingers along the ridge the succulent. "So, what about a cat?"

Keesha rolled her head back against the seat, "I don't want a cat."

"What? It looks like you have plenty of room for a cat box in the back. Just imagine," Jazmine snagged the mic and pretended to radio, "Breaker 1-90, my copilot, Pickles, spotted a bogey ahead so watch your speeds out there."

Keesha would spend days looking forward to truck stop picnics with her sister and niece, imagining all the stories she would tell, gathering little knick-knacks from gas stations to give to Dahlia, but as soon as they were together, the words would dissolve out from under her, cotton candy in a river. The important words, solid, meaningful words, were a wet clay she couldn't form quick enough to keep up with Jazmine. She managed to say, "living things—plants, kids, pets—that's *your* thing, Jazz. They're not my jam."

Still into the mic, Jazmine argued, "they could be—"

Dahlia yanked the mic from her mom and held it up to her mouth. She pressed the button and pantomimed talking, all the head wags, shoulder lifts, hand waves, and mouth movements of an animated monologue without a single sound.

"That's not how that works," Keesha said, forgetting to sign.

Jazmine laughed, "cut her some slack. She's never heard talking. She doesn't understand what we're doing with our mouths."

In admonishing the woman, Keesha feels abashed in the same way she had with Dahlia, as if she'd misunderstood a fundamental way other people operate in the world—as if she were the one with the strange gaps of knowledge. Seeming to sense Keesha's uncertainty, the woman cracks an eyelid, frowns, and leans toward Keesha, who is already pressed against the door, her own hand curled around the handle. "They. Hear. Our. Heartbeats."

"Right, of course," Keesha says, but doesn't let go of the handle.

The woman scans the sky through the windshield. She whimpers, presses the mic closer to the tendons threading her neck. Her eyes flutter and close, her head drops, and she folds up on herself. She warbles an upwelling of tears.

"Ah, Christ..." Keesha lets go of the door and puts a hand on the woman's bare shoulder. The skin rasps dry and ice cold under her fingers. The body trembles under her touch. "Hey, hey, let's not get worked up. Hey, I'll take you to Seward and we'll get you all taken care of."

"No," the woman wheezes through tears, but it's faint and Keesha senses a shift, a defeat she can exploit to finally shift everything into motion.

"It'll be fine."

"I'm not going back."

"Where is 'back'? Where did you come from?"

"I'm going to wait for Them. Even if...even if They don't come this time." She hiccups into a sob and bends her head almost to her knees.

"Oh, lady, hey, I bet whoever it is, they went to the police station to report you missing. And the police, they put out an ABP on you. Bet if I turn the dial to the right station, we can hear them looking for you."

The woman sits up again and shakes her head, "that's not how They are."

"How are they, then?"

"They come on their own time."

"Who are they?"

"They first came when I was young. Seventeen. Aiden was born. Raging. That kid was *born* angry. From the moment he came out, squalling, beet red, and his hands little fists. Oh, the crying...I just needed a rest," her voice drops out, "Joey was gone that night and in the field by the water tower...I had the shotgun...for the racoons and there was a—*shimmer*, all around and I was lifted. I felt *lifted*. Like, like I could breathe again." The cabin light clicks off. The moonlight silvers her eyes in the gloom. Her voice is a sandpaper rasp in the quiet of the cabin. The woman's story may have been weird, but it wasn't nonsense. It wasn't dementia. Despite the strangeness of the details, there was a certain *coherence* to the woman. "They want you to do things, but nothing is painful. Nothing is stressful. Every time I was with Them was like a vacation. I rested. True rest. Like sleeping *really* deep. It was the best I've ever been."

Keeping her eyes focused on the slow drift of cloud outside the window, Keesha thumbs through the index of her life and can't find a time she hadn't been hustling—working one job while studying to get licensed for the next job, counting pennies and tracking deposit days, negotiating with landlords, calculating every haul and every mile; now there was Dahlia, on the sidelines, about to be counted into the fast moving double-dutch of

Keesha's day-to-day life. Everything is scrambled and rucked-up with anxiety. She imagines what it would be like to walk into a clinic, give herself up to the white-clad nurses waiting to enfold her in an over-sized terry cloth robe, lead her into a quiet place called the soothing room, while someone else took care of the day-to-day of making-do. Keesha turns the cabin lights back on, the dimmer version that preserves the truck battery. "Sounds lovely. Why did you come back?"

"You don't get to pick how long They keep you. Gone for years. Gone for a day."

"Years? Gone for years? You're telling me you missed whole years of your life?"

"There wasn't much to miss. You miss paying bills? Miss the crying? Miss his noisy breathing as you're trying to watch TV?"

"No, nobody misses those things, but what about your kids, growing up."

"They learned to live with what I gave them."

Could kids learn to live on crumbs? Keesha only had a few signs, enough for a weekend aunt. Some rough sentences, the alphabet, a few jokes. Enough sign language to ask about the bathroom, get through a meal, but not enough to comfort Dahlia at night, half-awake, whimpering, and signing *mom mom mom mom mom* over and over again until Keesha couldn't bear it anymore and captured Dahlia's hands into quiet. How would she fit a sign language class into seventy hours on the road? It's not like there's a book on tape for sign language. Could Dahlia really grow into a healthy person feeding on the measly nutrients of Keesha's sign language?

Her niece as a spindly little weed growing up through broken concrete with Keesha's anemic signs. The woman's kids, yellow-headed dandelions in the same crack. "It couldn't have been easy for your kids."

"It was."

"No, I mean, kids need their momma."

The woman paused so long Keesha wondered if she'd heard. But she said so quietly Keesha had to lean into the sound, "it all went better when I was gone."

Keesha had to hold a hand over her heart for a moment to ease the constriction of her own grief. Outside, on their apartments' joint patio, Keesha negotiated babysitting rates and protocols with Lorena. Hard-smoking, ribbon-thin, epileptic Lorena with yellowed teeth and always-handy cart-on-wheels instead of a purse that ported her abundant day-to-day wares in her travels on the city busses. Her cheeks hollowed with each drag of cigarette. She motioned to Dahlia, a limpet attached to Keesha's waist. "I'm fine taking her for the week, hon, but what're you going to do when she goes back to school?"

"Back to school?"

"Yeah, she's in school, ain't she?

Keesha rubbed a hand over Dahlia's head, and her niece looked up. Keesha finger spelled, *Are you in school right now?*

Dahlia wrinkled her brow, glancing between Keesha and Lorena for the punchline to such an easy question. She signed, *yes*, then nodded vigorously.

Lorena scoffed, working herself into a cough. Keesha wanted to grab her already-packed travel bag, get in her truck and drive. Drive into the wilds of Canada. Somewhere she'd never been and couldn't find her way back from. Because even Lorena, with one son dead by suicide and the other a drug addict somewhere in Laredo, knew when a kid should be in school.

"Do you really think that's true? That they're better off without you?" Keesha asked the woman.

"I know they're better off without me, now. The shimmer will solve everything."

"Which is why you're out here, looking for a place where They can pick you up?"

When the woman smiles, Keesha sees the shine of teeth in the dim light.

"Lady, I get it...I get that it's something you believe, but—I just *can't* leave you out here."

The woman shifts in the seat. "People are afraid of Them, but They're not the ones who locked me in white rooms."

"Okay, but unless someone shows up—"

The cabin lights click off although no one touched them, and the woman is a mass of shadow across the seat, a dark cluster of matter that sucks up the air in the cabin. "I won't go."

"We can't sit here all night."

The woman screams.

"Shit!" Keesha claps her hands over her ears. In the tiny cabin of the truck, the unbroken howl amplifies to a painful reverberation. Keesha squeezes her eyes closed against the sight of the wide maw of the woman's mouth, ribbons of saliva, and teeth flashing between black spots of sounds and static. Keesha pleads, "Stop!"

The woman is right at Keesha's shoulder, quiet. Too close. Her proximity is aggressive, as if the woman is poised to bite her, disembowel her with long fingers.

"I won't go," the woman repeats, and she sounds like she did before food and conversation, the echo of the words doubling up in a sonic loop of each other.

"I won't force you anywhere, but can I at least radio in to my boss—" but the words squeeze quiet as pressure in the cabin deepens, as if molecules of air swelled wide. Keesha's stomach dips and her body presses into the seat with a squeak; then air just as quickly thins and Keesha lifts from the seat, as if gravity turned off. Every loosely anchored item—the mic, the hula girl on the dash, the can of Coke in the cup holder—rise too, spiraling into the space around them. Two seconds, maybe more, of weightlessness, and then gravity grabs them back. The Coke can clanks into the cup holder, the hula girl clatters to the dash, and Keesha whuffs out surprise.

Her left hand grips the door handle so hard it hurts, and her right hand bumps against her throat with the thread of air and pulsing blood. *Did I have a stroke?* The woman is unruffled, leaning forward to peer into the side mirror with atavistic focus.

Glancing in her own side mirror, Keesha sees a car parked behind her truck. A dark sedan, cool blue in the bend of northern lights, fins cresting the dark to shine in moonlight.

"Holy shit, where'd that car—"

"It's Them!" The woman is out of the cab instantly, passenger door left swinging open.

"Wait!" Keesha fights her own door handle, the simple mechanics stupefying her shaking hands. Leaping into the cold is like hitting a solid block, rattling her breath and heart so hard she leans against the truck for a moment to recuperate before dashing to the back. As she rounds the corner of the payload, she catches up to the woman where she's stopped a few feet from the nose of the sedan, arched low and still as a stick bug pretending to be a twig.

A driver and a passenger sit in the car, blocky shoulders and heads like drawings of shadows, framed in the pane of the windshield. Even night creatures have been stunned quiet, and the only sound besides the atmospheric movement of wind is their cooling engine pinging.

"Is that Them?" Keesha whispers.

The car headlights burst on, forcing Keesha back with a hand to shield her eyes against the bright blare. The woman stands her ground, and Keesha edges forward again, close enough to hear the woman keening a high-pitched sound wavering on the edge of a larger, louder ululation.

"Is that Them? Is this who you wanted?" Keesha considers breaking the intensity of the moment with a touch, but the woman has pinched her hands up close to her chest, so Keesha can't reach them without breaching the woman's space. Lit up by the beams, the woman's age-speckled skin is blown out bright white, darkened at ribs and hips by protrusions of bone. Motes flicker light to dark to light again, moving in and out of the lines of the headlights. A quivering point of eddying dark paints its way up the woman as a moth, out of season, hurls itself against the hard plastic of the mistaken moon.

A car door snicks open. The woman's keening stops.

Keesha can't hear or see movement past the cone of light, but the woman's head quirks as if following a sound.

"Hey, you're blinding us! Can you turn off your headlights?"

The lights tick off and the space fizzes into the cool air and soft light of the night. Through the blobs of after-burn, Keesha sees the driver is still seated behind the wheel, the passenger side empty. The Passenger stands at the nose of the car.

Wearing a black trench coat darker than the midnight blue of the evening, The Passenger is crisp, straight lines suggesting the shape of a female, and a wide-jawed moon face. Slicked back into a long, low ponytail, the Passenger's hair slithers against the shiny material of her coat as she turns her head first one way, then another.

"Moira, love, we're so glad you got in touch." The Passenger's voice is brimming with affection, honeyed, and happy.

Moira moves so fast Keesha isn't sure she sees it. For one moment, the woman is a potent, breathing, trembling creature close enough to touch and then, with a hard scrabble of foot against roadside rocks, she is yin-shaped white curled against the Passenger in a hug so tight the sinews of her arms flex.

The Passenger's coat squeaks as she encircles Moira in her arms, her black-gloved hands denting Moira's skin in firm embrace. Moira whimpers, and the sound could be relief or pain, but the Passenger murmurs nonsensical reassurances and Moira's eyes squeeze shut. "Tsk, Moira, love. It's okay now."

The Passenger lifts her eyes to Keesha. The precision of her hair, jacket, even the symmetrical arc of well-manicured eyebrows suggests officiousness. The confidence of competency and authority of officialdom, like all those Keesha has encountered who consider themselves in charge: doctors, police, the shabby chic social worker who kept insisting, "you're named in the will, but there are plenty of adoptive families who would be happy have a little girl like her." It's the I-know-what-to-do attitude that makes Keesha want to yield, trust the Passenger to handle Moira—but also resist, wondering not for the first time that night if she'd regret giving up so easily. If something went bad later and they saw her GPS, she could she say to the police, to Moira's family—but the woman *seemed* legit. No, not like any nursing home staff I've ever seen. No, not like a daughter or a niece.

"Who are you?" Keesha asks.

Very little on the woman's face moves when she speaks, but her head tilts left, then right. "Did Moira not tell you about us?"

"She talked about a 'them' and...I..."

"From the way she described us, you thought we would be little green aliens."

Keesha forced a quick laugh. *We're commiserating over Moira's specific delusion, right?* "Yeah, she certainly had a way of talking about you. I wasn't sure anybody would show up."

The Passenger shakes Moira gently, "Ah, we'd never fail our Moira."

"But, you did. I found her naked, wandering in the Alaskan cold. If you're supposed to be taking care of her, you've done a shitty job of it."

"*We* have always done a good job taking care of Moira," the Passenger insists. "It's the other people."

"Then who are you? What claim do you have on her?"

Moira's eyes flip open, a black opening in an expanse of pale face. "They're my family."

The Passenger reiterates, *"We're* her family."

Keesha knows they're not her family. Knows they don't resemble anything that could be easily construed as family. *So what now? Against her will, load her angry as a cat into my truck and take her to the police?* According to the Department of Transportation, Keesha's far enough beyond her Hours of Service that she would be in violation to drive her truck to Seward now. Her schedule is shot to shit. She's 2,382 miles from home, nine miles and hours from job done celebrated with a watery coffee and a Styrofoam plate of scrambled eggs with Tabasco at the Marina Motel. Add into that a police visit. Assuming a police station visit went well...A ragged long-haul trucker dragging a naked white lady into the station and an FBI-esque woman with easy solutions right behind.

Keesha looks away. The mist foams up from Bear Lake, the mountains jagged edges against the blue-black sky, and above it all the moon sunlight bright. It all seems too beautiful, too unreal to be true—like she's slipped sideways into a warped version of the world. She's a record player pressed to play slow, distorted sounds, the northern lights smeared as time and place slides around her. If it were daylight, if it were that chocolate lab with the collar on the side of the road and her ham and cheese sandwich as bait, if it had just been something straight, an old lady needing a ride home—maybe then she could have done it differently.

"It can't be this easy..." Keesha isn't sure even as she says it, "for me to trust her to you. To let her go."

The Passenger lifts her chin, her irises swell so wide her eyes go black and Keesha feels a buzzing, a vibrato of energy shimmying from her feet, up her legs, through fingers, palms, and chest, until it zips out the top of her head, lifting the roots of her hair. Her body feels wrought and loosened into jelly, as if all her ligaments were relaxed enough for muscle and bone to slip into piles if not for the skin holding them in.

"Jesus," Keesha gasps, and stumbles away from the car.

The Passenger's ponytail has cascaded across the crown of Moira's head, so Keesha can't see her eyes and can't see her mouth move, but when Moira speaks the sound feels close, like she's at her shoulder. "The shimmer."

"Stop!" Keesha points at the Passenger. "Don't you do anything to me."

"You're okay," the Passenger says so warmly, it tugs at Keesha.

"Don't *sweet talk* me."

The Passenger tsks. "We don't need to."

So softly she can't tell at first if it's just her eyes adjusting to the darkness, but the air around her lightens, the dark particles warming to a royal blue. Physically, Keesha has a sense of invite, a warm corona of welcoming. The shimmer envelopes. It soothes. Relief surges up hot and overwhelming, it's a reprieve. A break from the relentless future, the years of life without her sister. It feels as if her insides are being pulled up; a warm happy stretching of taffy. Her body lifts, eases up into the air until only her toes skitter across gravel.

The pull deepens, hip bones, shoulders, her right elbow angle upward, but her toes remain firm on the ground, like a counter-pull of tendon. A memory from the day before the trip becomes something integral to the inner-working of her body: Dahlia shadows Keesha as she packs her bag, watching every sock and shirt, every bra and jean. Just before Keesha zips it up she signals a frantic, *Wait!*, running out the bedroom, back in a flash with an armload of snacks, a banana, an apple, a box of animal crackers, a peanut butter and jelly sandwich that must have come from her own lunch earlier that day, and the Lego person. Dahlia nestles the treats into the folds of clothing in Keesha's duffel, but hands the Lego person directly to Keesha, signing, *it's a truck driver, like you! She can survive the dashboard.* Blue pants, a red shirt, bald head. As truck-driver looking as any Lego person could be. Dahlia's wide smile is a mile of over-sized teeth. Sadness clashes with delight, log jamming any decent response beyond, *thanks, kid,* as Keesha pockets the toy and almost runs to her truck.

Are those the last stupid words she'll have from me? Am I going to let her be some sad kid? Now the pull is painful, the anchored sinew and muscle stretched; she gasps, "no, no, let me go. I don't want to go into the shimmer."

"Fair enough," the Passenger says.

The sensation eases, the tingling of her scalp dissipating and her knees firming up under her. Every limb still tingles like she slept on them wrong and her lungs feel too small to bellow in all the oxygen she needs. Keesha bends and gulps big breaths. Moira is tucked under the Passenger's arm. The Driver is a man-shaped shadow in the car. They are all watching her.

"Moira, are you sure?" Keesha asks.

"Yes."

She isn't going to get Moira away from them. And she's not going with. She asks the Passenger, "what happens now? What do I tell my bosses? The cops? The people who come looking for her?"

The Passenger's voice is sweet, crystalized sugar crunched between teeth, but she's curt and confident. "You won't have to handle any of that. Don't worry. You get in your truck and go."

Keesha stumbles back around the driver's side of her truck, remembering too late that the passenger side door was left open. She hauls herself into her seat and the passenger door is closed.

Shaking so hard she can't stick the key into the ignition, it's a few tries before she can get the engine to turn. The cabin rumbles awake, hula girl bobbing, and the radio mid-song. Keesha clicks the automatic locks and blasts the heat. The blue of her dash is her world, the same gauges and glows for millions of miles. Now that she's, safe she feels supercharged—like Red Bull straight to her veins. She wishes she could peel out of there, leave them in a shower of pebbles and burnt rubber, but the truck lumbers forward, protests the way she hauls the wheel left to merge back on the road.

As she chugs up the hill, she looks back in the side mirror to see them, but everything reflected is jumpy moon and the snake of the blacktop, the chop of yellow dash down the middle of the road.

Her speed climbs, her engine shifting gears smoothly, and still she looks back and maybe she sees a blue glow on the horizon behind her. Maybe it's the northern lights. Maybe it's the mist of Bear Lake rising. Maybe it's nothing, and soon there's only dark and stars. She glances at her clock and it reads two minutes from when she stopped. The amount of time she's been back on the road already, but not the time she took to stop. Her watch, a digital Casio from her sister seven Christmases ago, shows the exact same time—the numbers flip to the next minute in sync. Never mind she always sets her watch five minutes fast.

Keesha doesn't pull over to the side of the road, she screeches the truck to a halt right there in the lane. She fumbles the phone out of her jacket pocket and starts calling her sister, phone to ear, the ringing of the line a comfort before she remembers and punches the red hang-up.

Keesha opens her door and flops out. Tears stream out of her eyes and she has to breath big and deep, relishing the electric cold zinging every bit of exposed skin, and her throat and lungs. The Lego trucker is in her hand, and she squeezes it hard, deep into the tendons of her hand, relishing the ache because it means she's awake, alive, and okay.

She's not sure how it will all look in daylight, what she'll say about what happened that night. What stories of the road she'll share, what stops she'll make, or what will come for her and Dahlia. Bent over in the cold, crying in relief and grief, she discovers all of the words are in her brain, a deep wide well of words, the lexicon of signs, the syntax of gestures and facial expressions of ASL, everything she'll need beyond *hey, kid,* but none of them enough to capture the enormity of what just happened.

The Pet Owner's Guide to Reptilian Hauntings

Jerica Taylor

Jerica Taylor was born in Maine in the winter, and consequently, is always warm. She is a chicken herder, former librarian, and Dana Scully devotee. She has an MFA from Emerson College. She lives with her wife and young daughter in Western Massachusetts.

Maggie does not have time for a lizard funeral. She has to drop Jason off at a bus stop half a mile away because of street repaving. She's agreed to open up at the library for Suparna for the whole month in trade for being able to leave early to take Jason to gymnastics while Kiersten's deployed. Toast takes too long, so she's eating jam on cold bread straight out of the refrigerator.

"Howard's dead!" Jason cries, and while Maggie feels a pang in her heart for her son, his dead pet gecko is just one more morning hurdle that means Maggie isn't going to have time to stop for coffee, or probably even put on mascara.

"It's ok, sweetie, let me see," Maggie says, gently guiding Jason away from Howard's terrarium. Howard is unmistakably dead. He's laying upside down, paws curled up like he's a dried beetle on hot pavement.

Maggie immediately blames herself for forgetting something important in Howard's care and feeding. His heat lamp is still on, but had she forgotten some supplement? It had been a terrible idea to get a new pet right before Kiersten left; animals were her wheelhouse. Maggie hugs her son, wipes his nose and encourages him to head downstairs and eat his cereal while she figures out what to do.

"We need to have a memorial service!" Jason moans from the stairwell. Kiersten's aunt passed away a few months ago, and they'd fought over whether or not to take Jason with them to the funeral. Maggie hadn't wanted to explain death to him yet, but Kiersten, in her matter-of-fact approach to feelings, had insisted it was crueler to pretend.

Maggie had honestly been more concerned about the physical details and the process of burial, but Jason had gone on and on about the commemoration with a kindergartner's super-powered over-focus.

"We can do a memorial service for him tonight," Maggie assures him. She hopes distantly that he'll forget, but Jason isn't an easily distracted baby without object permanence anymore.

"And FaceTime with Mimi!" That Kiersten was able to do videos at all was a luxury this deployment, but Maggie has business to discuss about the car and the deadline for Jason's next session of gymnastics, and she wants to tell her wife about her week. She does not want to televise a pet memorial.

"Ok," Maggie says. "Ok, tonight. Go eat your breakfast because we have to get you to school."

She feels cruel not offering to let him stay home through his grief, but she can't skip work. Maggie makes a note to check the pet store's adoption booklet to see if there's a refund for a death within a certain amount of time. Did small animals come with a money-back guarantee?

She covers Howard in the tank with a purple striped hand towel from the bathroom, offers a silent apology for his death and the indignity, and shuts the light to Jason's room. If she hurries, she can manage some dry shampoo.

Howard's memorial service that evening is thankfully brief, and Maggie's had a glass of wine, so it's easier to say what a good, kind gecko he was, even if they'd only had him for a few weeks. They can't get ahold of Kiersten, who is likely on a training exercise, but the attempt seems enough to soothe Jason.

Howard goes into a shoe box, the sacrificed towel a warm blanket, and Jason spends a long time collecting stones from the tank that he thinks Howard would like to put in alongside him.

Maggie manages to convince Jason he can't stay up for them to bury Howard in the backyard since it's already an hour past his bedtime. She sorely wishes Kiersten were home, because this sort of thing is easier with two parents. And Kiersten could actually dig a hole pretty fast.

Standing in the dark with a flashlight propped on the picnic table to dig a grave for a pet lizard at 11:00 P.M. after eating her kid's leftover, cold grilled cheese for dinner... is definitely not one of the highlights of parenthood. The night is weirdly still; Maggie can't remember the last time she was outside this late. Back when she and Kiersten still lived in Boston, maybe, coming back from dinner with friends, or maybe it was a concert. She feels a pang for the sound of the traffic, the bus line that ran along their old street.

She bids Howard goodbye, feeling awkward about not saying more, even though she had yet to form a real attachment to him. He was a good gecko, as far as she knows about geckos, and she's sorry he died in her care. After covering his tiny grave, she remembers the bag of live crickets she'd just bought. She wishes them well on their second chance at life as she releases them into the dark yard, the grass already wet with dew.

The next morning is when things really get weird.

"Mommy, where's Robot Rancher?"

Maggie's pretty sure this isn't the first time Jason's shouted the question at her, but paused in front of the kitchen counter, carton in her hand, ready to pour milk in her coffee, she can't answer.

There's a ghost gecko sitting next to her coffee cup. Not a random gecko. It has to be Howard. Howard's ghost, head up, like it always when he was waiting for a treat. She is certain he's somehow come back to life, until the sunlight hits him and he's slightly translucent.

"Mommy!"

"Just a second, hon," Maggie calls, her voice unsteady.

Robot Rancher is in his usual place, wedged under the ottoman that Jason pretends is Robot Rancher's Robot Tractor. Maggie finishes her coffee in the living room, watching Jason spray cereal milk all over the iPad screen when he laughs at a fart joke. Much to her dismay, Howard's ghost is still sitting on the counter when she goes back for a coffee refill.

Maggie reaches out, hand trembling, to touch him. Her fingers pass right through him and he disappears.

Maggie goes to work and tells herself she imagined the whole thing, that she hasn't gotten enough sleep and she's getting paranoid with Kiersten gone. Maybe she's more disturbed by the death than she let herself believe.

When she comes home, Jason abandons his shoes and backpack and launches himself onto his sensory swing with a comic book Maggie brought home from the new releases shelf.

Howard's ghost is sitting on the edge of the couch in the living room where he was never allowed. Kiersten had been worried about the gecko's pads getting pet hair or debris. Maggie was more concerned about the gecko getting lost forever in the living room furniture.

"Hi," Maggie says tentatively. Howard blinks at her.

Do you feed a ghost pet?

Maggie had moved Howard's tank out of Jason's room and into the basement, hoping that he wouldn't be unnecessarily reminded of the loss. She goes down and gets a scoopful of dried meal worms and scatters them on the couch.

"Ewwww," Jason says as he finds the worms after dinner. "Mommy!"

Maggie cleans up the worms with the Dustbuster under the watchful eye of Howard's ghost while Jason crushes graham crackers unseeing under his sock feet.

The adoption booklet unsurprisingly does not have a section covering when your pet dies and becomes a ghost. All it covers is how to get a replacement gecko; though, in all honesty, if Jason had been a little younger, she probably would have done just that and convinced him the new gecko was Howard after a very successful check-up with the lizard doctor.

Howard's ghost is eyeing her from the atop the refrigerator. She tries ignoring him, but it is easier said than done. She feels his unblinking eyes following her, telegraphing the dreaded moment when he would leap for her and start climbing with his tiny suction feet.

Maggie doesn't believe in ghosts, but she also doesn't believe she's tired enough to hallucinate. At work, she googles 'ghost pets' and 'ghost-like phenomenon' and 'lizards after death' and counts it in her reference desk daily question statistics.

Maggie belongs to a Facebook Mom's group of alums from college that probably wouldn't throw her out if she posted asking if anyone had ever had a pet come back as a ghost. But it was the sort of place you asked for collective advice on investing or favorite convertible car seats, so she's probably better off keeping it to herself.

Instead, half-hopeless, she turns to Google again. "Can a pet come back as ghost?" turns up plenty of "It happened to me!" stories and a Reddit thread about haunted objects which only adds to her paranoia. It's the wrong question anyway. Maggie knows a pet can come back as a ghost. She's being watched by Howard in her kitchen right now.

Finally, Maggie ends up at a YouTube channel of night-vision-filled videos of people exploring abandoned buildings in the county. It's suspenseful and full of jump cuts and has zero useful information about her very real problem. She watches enough that when she tries to fall asleep, all she sees is Howard lurking behind a corner of her bedside table in dim green light.

Why is Howard haunting her? Why her and not Jason? Does Howard's ghost know, like Jason, like all small creatures, that it's better to seek out a grown-up, even from the spirit world? Even worse, is Howard expecting her to know what to do?

Maggie's trying to find the day bed under the piles of unfolded laundry she dumped on it to fold later when she hears Jason wake up shouting for her. She's almost folded all the towels – by far the easiest load – and she resigns herself to the fact that even those aren't going to get done anytime soon.

Jason is sitting up in bed, dry sobs and hiccups wracking his chest under Spider-man pajamas.

"Did you have a nightmare?"

Jason shrugs. Maggie winces as he opens his mouth wide in what she's expecting to be a scream. Instead it turns into a yawn. "I miss Howard," Jason sniffles.

"I know you do, sweetie." She wishes she could tell her son Howard is still around, if not exactly in the same way. "It's so sad when we lose a pet we love. But just think of him on the other side of the rainbow bridge."

Jason leans into her shoulder, eyes already closing again. "That's the bridge to animal heaven, right?"

"It is. Howard crossed the bridge and now he's meeting all sorts of other new friends."

"And he's happy?"

She looks around at Jason's room, his nearly flattened beanbag chair, his stuffed dinosaurs sprawled out on the floor like a meteor had struck.

Promising that Howard is happy in a magical pet afterlife feels like a sharp lie while he is downstairs haunting their kitchen. She fears his spirit is still lingering because he's vengeful, but could a vengeful gecko really do any harm?

"He's happy," Maggie says, and kisses the top of Jason's head, willing it to be true.

By the middle of the week, Maggie has a headache she can't shake. After an off-site training on a new feature of the cataloging system that was more mind-numbing than educational, she loops around back home. She'll tell work that the training ran late or the school called and Jason had a fever. Whatever. She just needs a few hours to herself, dozing on the deck, maybe reading the mystery novel before it's due back.

No, she'd stopped reading that one when a ghost appeared to the heroine.

A nap. She'll definitely try a nap before she has to go pick up Jason. It's another moment she sorely misses Kiersten. On a day like this, she could ask Kiersten to pick up dinner on her way back from the base. Kiersten could do bedtime. Kiersten could hug her firmly and reassure her that she saw the ghost of their son's pet gecko, too.

There's a strange car in the driveway, and Maggie's heart soars with hope that Kiersten's home early, and maybe someone gave her a ride, or the car didn't start and she got a rental. Her hope tells her wild stories, all of them believable if it means her wife could be here now and Maggie wouldn't have to handle anything else alone.

Instead of Kiersten, a woman with gray hair caught up in a frizzy bun is crouched in the driveway, uncoiling an orange extension cord dangling from Maggie's kitchen window.

"Excuse me," Maggie says. She almost forgets to shut off her car as she jumps out to demand this woman explain what she's doing.

"Oh, hello dear," the woman says. Now that Maggie is closer, she can see that the extension cord is plugged into something that looks like an air compressor with a couple of mason jars attached. "Would you believe I work for the gas company?"

"Well, the gas meter is on the other side of the house, and not in my kitchen, so no."

"How about Animal Control?"

"I think you lost your chance to lie with the first question."

The woman nods, agreeing that yes, she has been caught out in a lie and remains entirely unfazed.

Maggie vacillates between awkward and furious. She doesn't need this. She has a headache and she has to solo parent for the next six months and she has a ghost pet in her house and this stranger doesn't even have the good grace to pretend to be ashamed she's been caught doing something bizarre.

The woman turns on the air compressor thing. It revs like a car engine failing to turn over, and then it whistles like Maggie's pressure cooker when she's too impatient and goes for the manual release.

"Alright then," the woman says, content with her examination of her equipment. "My name's Agatha, and I'm here for your ghost."

Tears spring to Maggie's eyes and she angrily wipes them away. Howard is real. This is the most absurd thing that has ever happened to her.

"You're here for the ghost gecko?"

"Oh, is it a reptile. I see. We were wondering, it appeared to be quite small."

"It was my son's. They're palm sized. His name is – was – Howard. Wait, who are you? Who's we?"

"The simplest answer," Agatha says, "is that we are cleaners."

It is simple. Elegantly simple. Agatha has come here to clean her home of a ghost.

"How did you know I had a ghost? Were you tracking my internet browsing history?"

"I wouldn't know how to do that, dear. No, we have these machines that can read energy signatures. In my day, we used gifted people, but I do have to say the machines are much more accurate and can give you an address. The hours I spent knocking on people's doors pretending I was from the town census. I did get a lot of people registered to vote that way, though," she says, looking thoughtfully up at the clouds.

"So you can – you can take him away? Howard? The ghost?"

Agatha nods, and then fiddles again with her ghost cleaning machine as it makes a few plaintive beeps.

"Do you know why he's here?" She's embarrassed at her voice shaking.

"This is where he lived, right?" Agatha asks. "This is where he died?"

"Yes, of course, but I mean, why is my son's pet gecko a ghost?"

Agatha shrugs as if Maggie's asked about the weather and not an existential question about life, death, and existence. "You'd have to ask him."

"I did!" Maggie bursts out. She asked as she fried Jason an egg and Howard eyed her from on top of the coffeemaker. When his tail draped over the keyboard of her laptop like he was trying to get warm. When he stared at her from the mail sorter as she grabbed her keys to leave each morning. "I asked if he had unfinished business, and if he had been happy, or if he was sad he had died. I asked everything I could think of." To her relief, Agatha's expression isn't one of judgment, but quiet consideration.

"Well," Agatha says. "I imagine he might not know, either. Even as a ghost, he's still only a lizard."

All this time, Maggie's been thinking Howard had some mission, some reason for being there – a haunting agenda. She'd carried the guilt of whatever had gone wrong, the grudge Howard held against them, or his fate. She hadn't done enough for her son and she hadn't done enough for his lizard and everything was on her shoulders. It's possible that the whole time Howard has been as confused as Maggie is.

"This thing you're doing, it's going to remove him?" Maggie gestures at the air compressor.

"It will remove and contain the energy that is his ghost," Agatha says. "We use EMF as well as light-and-heat sensitive equipment to identify a before and after reading." Maggie can't process most of what Agatha is saying. She's letting this strange woman vacuum away a ghost reptile but she needs to know that it will all be ok.

"Will he be happy?" Her breath hitches and two hot tears spill down her cheeks and trail down her chin. She wipes at them with her sleeve. She thinks of what she promised Jason; Howard the gecko on a hot rock in the sun in heaven, eyes bright.

"If you're asking if he will achieve eternal rest, I don't know," Agatha says. "I can tell you this. I've worked with ghosts for most of my life, and they're not the same as the living individual, people or pet. They're a sort of after-image. So while your son's pet gecko may appear to still be here, his soul, or whatever made him who he was, will forever be intangible and unfathomable."

Maggie's ashamed tears are still falling. She takes a deep, shaky breath.

"Grief is good, my dear," Agatha says, gently patting Maggie's arm. "Sure sign you're still alive. You can go along inside, pour yourself a glass of water. I'll be done here in just a moment."

"Am I supposed to pay you something?"

Agatha's laugh is like a cat jumping on piano. "No," is all she says.

"Thanks," Maggie says. "For taking care of him." It's still there, in her words, that she hopes this woman and her cleaning and her energy reading equipment will send Howard on to wherever he's supposed to be.

All thoughts of a nap are gone, even though Maggie feels exhausted. She tidies the mail on the counter, checks the school lunch menu for next week. She's afraid to see Howard's ghost disappear, sucked away, but she doesn't see him at all. Maybe he's already gone.

The whistling of Agatha's device winds up and down several times before finally going quiet, and Agatha looks up to wave farewell to Maggie through the fingerprint-smeared window, but she's not saying goodbye, she's asking Maggie to unplug the extension cord. Maggie hasn't even asked how she got inside in the first place. She wiggles the orange cord loose from the outlet and Agatha winds it up. Maggie would like to say she doesn't search the house for signs of Howard once Agatha's car disappears down the street, but she does. She doesn't find anything paranormal anywhere.

Kiersten calls at 3:00 A.M., and by some miracle, Maggie hears the phone and answers.

"Hi babe, I can't believe you're awake. I know it's sometime ridiculous time-"

"3:14," Maggie says to crow as loud as possible to Kiersten, who laughs.

"I'm glad you answered."

"Me, too."

They catch up on household matters, Jason's struggles in science, and the schedule for Kirsten's return before coming around to the matter weighing most heavily on Maggie's mind.

"So, should we get him another gecko?" Kiersten asks. "You can put him off till I'm home, and I can go with him."

"Grandma Pam actually mentioned she has your Dad's old bird cage."

"So you're firmly anti-reptile?"

"No, if that's what he really wants, fine," Maggie says, though she doesn't really mean it. She'd still try to talk him out of it. "It was a bit traumatizing, to have it die so soon. You didn't have to prepare its coffin." *You didn't see its ghost for a whole week before some oddball, kind old lady sucked it away with a supernatural vacuum,* she thinks.

"Pets die," Kiersten says matter-of-factly. It's so Kiersten that Maggie smiles into the cradle of the phone. "That's just part of being a pet owner. We're always going to outlive them."

She thinks of Kiersten stationed on the other side of the world. The one time she got a call from her superior officer that Kiersten had received a concussion from friendly fire. The terror that shot through her. If Kiersten died, would her ghost haunt the house, or would be it be bound to some mobile med-tent in Afghanistan? Would someone like Agatha – a cleaner - have to come along to put her to rest?

"Hey, you ok?" Kiersten says.

"Yeah, yeah, just sleepy," Maggie lies.

"Ok, well then go back to sleep. We'll talk about pets when I get home. I'll tell Jason when I email him that I want him to wait so I can choose something new with him."

"Thanks," Maggie says. "Be safe."

"Love you," Kirsten says.

"Love you," Maggie echoes, though the call's already disconnected in far-away static. "You, too, Howard," she says. She doesn't, really; if anything, she only got fond of him when he was a ghost. But if he had an eternal soul, it was a lizard's eternal soul, and maybe a little bit of belated not-quite-love could go a long way to whatever rock he rested on, lux aeterna.

Keep Moving

Raluca Balasa

Raluca Balasa is a fantasy and science fiction author from the Toronto area. Despite the dark nature of most of her stories, she has a soft spot for inter-species friendships and birds.

Today Sarrai had to move again. She'd stopped asking why; the explanation was always the same. People form emotional attachments by proximity, and a smart girl should have learned by now that those can kill you. The trick is to keep moving, young lady. Always keep moving.

If she pressed the matter, she'd get another history lesson. Those never varied much, either. Before the child-rearing institutions, children had only two caregivers, the male and female who were also their lifegivers. They had siblings, other children who lived with them all the time, and were under a spell called *love* that made them hurt when the others did. In the early days after Arasu's Plague, lifegivers had cried themselves to death over harsh words exchanged with their offspring. Men had stopped breathing when separated from their mates. Even now, with all the precautions taken, danger lurked around every corner. Just last week, a merchant had a heart attack while arguing with a customer. Would she like that, because that was what relationships did. The commoners of Calibei were a gentle, sensitive people since the Plague, and if she didn't start packing her things this instant she wouldn't get any dessert.

So she packed, and together with forty-nine randomly-assigned children, started the march toward the next institution. This one was halfway across the city. The sun blazed brightly today, and everyone carried umbrellas in addition to the scarves draped over their heads. The instructors had forced Sarrai to put on a visor so the brightness wouldn't blind her, but now she couldn't see much of anything at all. She kept tripping over her feet.

"Are you thirsty, child? Is it the heat?" came the instructor's voice. Sarrai wasn't allowed to know the instructors' names before her tenth nameday, when she'd apparently be emotionally stable enough to handle such intimacy without getting attached. She squinted up where she thought the instructor's face might be.

"It's not hot, and I can't see."

"Ah, you need a darker visor."

"A lighter one."

The instructor paused. "That's enough trouble from you, young lady. Come along."

Hands pushed her into motion again. Sarrai sighed but said nothing. She could just yank this thing off when no one was looking, but they'd only force her to put it on again. They didn't know that every time she went out to do her chores, she didn't wear one. She didn't need to cover her skin, either; the sun didn't burn her like it did everyone else. When it thundered outside, she didn't wear earplugs, and she doubted a simple argument would –

The queue stopped. People started muttering, and Sarrai pulled off her visor without thinking in her haste to see what was happening. The motion yanked down her head scarf, too, but she barely noticed.

A man in uniform stood ahead, speaking with one of the instructors. He was big, broad-shouldered, at least a head taller than the instructor. He wore no visor, no scarf, and his skin was golden rather than the milky white of everyone else on the street. She'd heard about the Imperial soldiers being giants, but she'd thought that a figure of speech.

"You can't pass this way." He spoke loudly, not in that whispering voice most people used. The instructor winced as if he'd shouted. "The road's closed."

"Is there danger?"

The soldier frowned. As a direct relative of the emperor, he didn't have to answer to anyone but the governor. The road was closed if he said so and that was that – but after a moment, his face softened and he muttered, "We've had reports of a rogue Siren."

"Arasu have mercy," breathed the instructor. Some of the younger children started crying. The instructors ushered them together and turned them around, and Sarrai let her visor drop from her numb fingers as she followed. Was there really a Siren out there? She'd never seen one, but legend had it they were Arasu's chosen people, here to bring pain to those the devil-goddess hated. The terrible sounds they made could drive a man mad with grief or make him laugh until he died. She shuddered thinking about it.

"Quickly, children, quickly!" shouted the instructors, nearly tripping over the long hems of their dresses as they ran. You didn't want to be caught within hearing-range of a Siren. Sarrai reached for her earplugs, but someone jostled her and she dropped them. Her pounding heart mingled in her ears with the trampling of feet.

And then she heard it.

A soft, trilling sound, like the calls she'd once heard from a bird at her windowsill. Back then she'd thought she was dreaming

– everyone knew birds were bred without vocal chords – but she had no doubt about this sound now. It moved with purpose, with power. It lifted something from Sarrai's heart even as the children around her shrieked and wailed. It was a sad sound, yes, but Sarrai ached in a way that didn't hurt, if that made any sense. The pain felt...human. She tried to slow, but an instructor grabbed her hand and hurried her forward until the sounds stopped vibrating in the air.

It didn't matter. They continued vibrating in Sarrai's ears, her heart. For the first time since she could remember, she felt alive.

***

Feet paced outside her room. They'd been doing that for hours. Sarrai went to the door and peered through the keyhole again. The two instructors who'd been muttering together had become a group of at least eight. They looked like giant bats, all swathed with fabrics to avoid exposing their sensitive skin to the elements. As if there were any "elements" indoors. Sarrai slumped down with her back against the door, fighting back tears.

So she'd taken off her visor. Big deal! That was no reason not to feed her all day, or to lock her in a dark and lonely room away from all signs of life. It wasn't like she'd caught some disease – was it? Were her eyes infected from the sun? Fear pumped through her again, but she refused to cry because she couldn't hear the instructors' whispers over her blubbering when she did. She wiped her nose on her sleeve and strained her ears, pressing her face to the door. It was made of smooth petrified wood; regular wood gave off splinters no matter how polished it was. People were such big crybabies. She wouldn't be like that.

"...no head scarf. The girl should have been affected by sunstroke within minutes. We traveled for a half hour before I noticed the state she was in. She didn't even seem *aware* that her eyes and head were unprotected! Look at her face. No sunburns, nothing at all.

"She told me her visor was...too dark."

Gasps. Sarrai scoffed to herself.

"And the Siren's song didn't frighten her. She didn't seem to be in pain at all."

"Is it possible...?"

"No. Don't think it. There's no way we could have made such a mistake."

"We *have* to think it, Semisola. The consequences could be grave if this goes uncorrected. Who collected her from her lifegivers seven years ago?"

"The records name an Instructor Aduvari."

"Bring him."

***

It took three days for Instructor Aduvari to arrive from the other end of town. The two head instructors whose names she'd learned were Semisola and Neera awaited him in one of the spare classrooms. Sarrai stood in the corner; Semisola had insisted she be here so they could cross-reference her features with those of her lifegivers. Whatever that meant.

Aduvari studied the papers in his hands, looking from them to Sarrai and back again. Sarrai had never liked being the center of attention. Now she just wanted to sink into the ground. The instructors' gazes bore into her with scrutiny.

"She certainly resembles the woman," Aduvari murmured, stroking his chin. "And she has her father's eyes. It's their child, no doubt. She's the baker's daughter – nothing more, nothing less."

"But she has the royal strength, Instructor," said Neera in her nasal voice. "I bore witness to it. The sun doesn't hurt her and neither does music. Perhaps a royal baby went missing seven years ago and the baker found her? She could be the governor's own daughter, for Arasu's sake! We *must* investigate."

All three pairs of eyes latched on Sarrai again. She struggled not to squirm. "Do you consider yourself special, girl?" Aduvari asked. His beard was so long he tucked it into his belt. Trembling, Sarrai shook her head. She'd never thought of herself as *special* so much as normal. Was normalcy special when you were the only normal person around?

"Have you no tongue?" Aduvari demanded.

Sarrai stepped forward. "Apologies, Instructor. I've never considered myself anything."

Aduvari nodded, but he looked displeased. Neera and Semisola shared glances. Before she could stop herself, Sarrai blurted, "What did I say?" and all three instructors winced.

"She speaks loudly," Semisola muttered. "Like the Imperial soldiers."

Sarrai's fear turned into an urge to laugh. She certainly wouldn't discourage the notion that she was royalty, if they wanted to believe that, but how could such a small-boned, pale, timid creature like herself be related to the emperor and his bronze men? Imperial soldiers were fearless, strong of body, heart, and mind. Sarrai was too shy to even ask for seconds at dinner. It had taken her years to work up the courage to remove her visor when she went out alone, even though she'd known she didn't need it. Part of her had been terrified her eyeballs would become scorching cinders in her head as soon as the sunlight struck them. For years she'd lived in a dull, colorless world of whispers and shadows because of it.

The Imperial soldier I saw today didn't need a visor. I've always known I was strong of body like them. Maybe the heart and mind parts can be learned.

"Have you tried feeding her milk?" Neera was saying. "We'll see if she's lactose tolerant."

"I wouldn't want to make the child sick..."

"That's a small price to pay for our peace of mind."

"The governor will suspect something when we request *milk* from the garrison's provisions, Sola –"

Royalty! Sarrai couldn't help smiling. They would send her to the citadel to train as an Imperial soldier, and she'd be allowed to do whatever she wanted without anyone breathing down her neck. She'd learn to protect both herself and the district of Calibei with sword and shield. There would be no more whispering, no more swathing herself in fabrics, no more squinting to read in the dark, no more tasteless foods.

"Take her directly to the governor. He can test her at the citadel."

***

Sarrai gathered the three long dresses she owned and stuffed them into the leather rucksack she normally used to rotate from one institution to the next. Her insides squirmed with excitement and trepidation.

In another year, she would have had to pick a trade and start her apprenticeship. She'd actually been considering becoming a baker, for Arasu's sake. She would have gone back to her lifegiver without even knowing it. It had been a brilliant idea of hers to liven up the food around here by slipping in a few extra ingredients, but now that she knew she was royal, she was glad she hadn't done it. She could've made people sick. She was different from them – stronger. Royal. A bastard daughter of the king's second cousin, perhaps, but still! She laughed to herself and continued packing. The instructors had let her open her windows, and the sun blazed brightly into her room, warming her bedsheets. She wanted to jump into bed and roll in them, but the instructors had told her to hurry. The coach would be here any minute to take her to the governor's citadel.

Without these soundproofed windows closed, Sarrai could hear the sounds of Calibei as people bustled in the streets. There weren't many – just feet, the occasional voice, and the wind – but to Sarrai they seemed to have a sort of harmony. The wind was clear and high-pitched, reminding her of that trilling sound she'd heard from the Siren. Someone beat a rug in half-time to the wind, and a boy carrying two water jugs ran in double-time. The sounds coursed through her like the blood through her veins. Every part of her ached to touch them, to join them. She left her rucksack and began beating on the windowsill like the carpet-beater, then added more beats when she realized she could while still keeping time. She just had to make them shorter. A smile touched her lips.

Then a thought struck her. What if she used her voice to imitate the wind? Sometimes, when she was alone, she would imitate the sound of the crackling fire or scraping chair, but they were just sounds. The wind's noise was something different, more like an equation. It made *sense*.

Sarrai listened for another moment. She could do it. Now that she was royal, she didn't have to be quiet anymore. She took a deep breath.

And alone in her room, she sang.

***

It could have been minutes. It could have been hours. Sarrai had gotten so lost in the music that she didn't remember herself until a booted foot kicked down her door. She yelped, whirling around so suddenly she nearly fell out the window. The two Imperial soldiers facing her had chiseled jaws and low, heavy brows and eyes that narrowed at the sight of her. They wore high-collared, sleeveless tunics belted at the waist with leather.

Behind them, Instructor Semisola sobbed into her hands.

Fear gripped Sarrai so powerfully she couldn't move. One of the soldiers stomped toward her and grabbed her arm, forcing her away from the window. His fingers were impossibly strong, and for the first time in her life, Sarrai felt her flesh bruise. Tears streamed down her face as he took a long piece of cloth from his pocket.

"Please don't," she pleaded, cringing away from him. "I haven't done anything! I'm – I'm royal!"

"Don't let it speak," said the second soldier, who Sarrai noticed kept a wary distance from her. "It will put a spell on you. Gag it."

She opened her mouth to plead again, but the soldier holding her struck her across the face. She fell to the ground, dazed. A powerful hand lifted her and forced the gag on so tightly she felt it cutting the corners of her mouth. Then the soldier grabbed her by her hair and forced her out of the room.

***

"Did you hear what the hellspawn said, Malik?"

The carriage moved smoothly on Calibei's paved roads toward the governor's citadel. Sarrai's eye had swollen shut, her lips had cracked from thirst. The soldier named Malik forced a chuckle but made no other response. He still held his hand on the pommel of his sword, though his companion had hung his weapon – sheath and all – upon the wall. Sarrai had spent the last three hours plotting how best to grab it with tied hands the next time one of them stopped to relieve themselves.

"Said she was *royal*," the first soldier continued. "Fancies herself our kin." He turned a steely gaze on Sarrai. "You are the devil's daughter, Siren. The Imperial soldiers are man's protectors – your kind, man's torturers. Do you enjoy causing pain? Is that why you do it?"

Sarrai just stared back at him, tired of trying to negate accusations she didn't understand. If she could speak, she would have screamed, "Do *what?*" ten times already, but they wouldn't even take off the gag to give her water. Her face felt very dry from the salt in her tears. She wished she hadn't cried so much. Maybe she would've been less thirsty now.

"Leave it be," Malik muttered. "Don't bait it. The governor will discipline it as he sees fit."

It. In the blink of an eye, she'd gone from royalty to a monster undeserving of the most basic human titles. It didn't make sense; how could she be a Siren? She didn't want to hurt anyone, and she didn't think what she did with her voice was hideous. How could it hurt others when it made her feel so peaceful? Was it true, then? Did she like causing pain?

"It watches my sword, Malik." The words jolted Sarrai out of her reverie. "It's a survivor. These types usually are."

She averted her eyes, though she knew they'd already seen her looking and, worse, read the fear of being caught on her face. Malik tightened his grip on his pommel, but the other just laughed. "Worry not, little beast," he said. "You'll have your chance to fight. After the governor cuts out your tongue, he'll put you in the ranks and send you to war. Sirens are placed anywhere deemed too dangerous for an Imperial soldier to venture. Our lives are too precious to waste, but yours..."

"Quiet!" hissed Malik.

"Would you be more comfortable on patrol duty, my friend? Or back in the capital, hiding behind your mother's skirts?"

"You're a fool to taunt Arasu's Chosen–"

"Ah, I *told* Koph you fret like a commoner –"

The carriage jumped suddenly, throwing Sarrai from her seat. She tumbled into the soldiers and all three fell to the ground in a tangle of fabric and chains. The carriage leaned heavily to the right as if a wheel had come off; Sarrai could hear the driver yelling somewhere far away. Her head swam with pain – had she hit it? – but a primal part of her stored that information for later. Injury didn't matter now. The carriage was tilting both her and the soldiers toward the door.

She grappled for the handle, but a hand clamped her ankle and dragged her back. The jumping wood beat her body mercilessly; these benches weren't rounded like the ones at the institution, and they had no cushions. She felt her gag slip down her neck as the soldier pulled her back toward him. The driver slowed and soon the carriage came to a halt, and without the confusion of motion, Sarrai knew she had lost. One of the soldiers came behind her, grabbed her about the waist, lifted her and threw her back onto the bench. She couldn't hold out her hands to stop her fall, and pain erupted in her body from the contact with the hard wood. The other soldier cursed under his breath.

Facedown on the bench, angry and terrified, Sarrai did the only thing she could think of – the thing that came more naturally than running, fighting or crying. She used her voice. Despite the wild pounding of her heart and the ringing in her ears, it came out clear. It didn't shake like her body did, and she realized after a few moments that she was repeating what she'd heard from the Siren all those days ago. She recalled every note, the way they interacted with and answered each other, every fluctuation in beat. Alone they were nothing, but together these sounds meant something. One day she would figure out what.

The soldiers didn't scream out in pain. They did nothing at all. Sarrai started to wonder if they'd run away or just dropped dead at her feet, but she couldn't convince herself to turn around. Sirens weren't supposed to be capable of hurting royalty. She remembered that now.

So what were they doing?

Slowly, carefully, she turned. The soldiers faced her, swords dangling by their sides in loose grips, identical expressions of puzzlement on their faces. They didn't seem to be in physical pain, but one of them – Malik – had tear tracks down his cheeks. Both looked pale and weak. She *was* hurting them, she realized.

And this thing that gave them pain made her happier than she could ever remember being. She *was* a monster.

Without looking back, Sarrai slipped out the window and ran.

***

The baker was not a horned, scaly beast, and the evilest thing about him was a tendency to overeat. Sarrai knew, had been watching him for weeks. He had a large belly and smiled at everyone who entered his store. The monster must have come from her mother's side, but it would be impossible to track her down without snooping into the public records, which were kept away from all but royal eyes. It didn't matter. She was what she was, and knowledge wouldn't change that.

Another mating season had come and gone, and today a woman came into the shop with a baby in her arms. Both lifegivers had to be present to sign papers and formally give the child over to the empire. The mother looked anxious; she had already grown attached to it. Sarrai didn't see why. From the glimpse she'd caught up in the trees, it looked like a mix between a rodent and a monkey. Had she been that ugly as a baby?

The door closed behind the mother, and the people from the child-rearing institution arrived a short while later. Sarrai couldn't see much through the window – they kept it so dark inside – so she waited until the door opened again and two forms stepped past the threshold.

"Sunrise tomorrow," one of them called back to the baker. Then they pulled up their visors, wrapped the scarves around their heads, and were gone. As soon as they were out of sight, Sarrai jumped down from the tree and yanked on her visor. She didn't want to stand out – not here, anyway.

She entered the baker's shop.

He emerged from the backroom, wiping his hands on his apron. He looked up at her, smiled. It was the same smile he gave everyone, and Sarrai had expected nothing else. She smiled back at him.

Then she started singing.

After he'd run from the shop, clutching his ears and sobbing so hard he could barely draw breath, Sarrai entered the backroom and went directly to the cot with the black bundle on it. Black meant it was a boy. The thing made hardly a sound when she approached it, and cooed softly when she picked it up. A spit bubble vibrated at the corner of its mouth, and it squirmed as if it were trying to escape its own skin.

But it wasn't crying. It would be a monster like her.

Sarrai held the baby to her, felt the life emanating from it. Imperial soldiers would come after this boy as they'd come after her, but she would never let them have him. Even monsters needed a little protection. The trick was to keep moving, to just keep moving until your transience became as natural as the changing seasons and no one thought to ask about you any more than they thought to ask why summer turned to fall. Finally, now that she had someone to move for, Sarrai understood.

The Devil and Dice

Diana Hurlburt

Diana Hurlburt is a librarian and writer in Florida. Selections of her short fiction can be found at Kaaterskill Basin, Body Parts, cahoodaloodaling, and The Hanging Garden, and in the anthologies Beyond the Pillars and Equus.

Upon Orca and Dice Enright's birth, Pastor Papa took one look at them and declared they'd been formed in the bellies of God and the Devil, brought together to swell Willa Enright's abdomen only by ease and circumstance, for how were God and the Devil to give birth on this mortal plane save for the casual, swift usage of a human woman's parts? It was women's purpose, after all. Pastor Papa didn't beam over the births—he saved his smiles for Sunday—but he laid one hand on each girl's forehead and decreed them the fulfillment of a prophecy long told. "Twins," he intoned, eyes glowing, and Willa figured she'd gone feverish with the birth, "twins are a holy thing, and an evil one. Oh yes indeed! There is a twin for above"—meaning God—"and one for below. This is the word of the Lord."

It wasn't no word to be found in Willa's Bible, but Pastor Papa's word was the law in Gibbs, Florida.

Someone stuck paperwork under Willa's sweaty hand, demanded legal names for the county register, the name of their father. *Orca? Dice? What kind of names for beautiful little girls—*

Willa shrugged. Said the best weekend of her life had been in Orlando watching the big black whales at SeaWorld, playing games at the Vegas-themed bar downtown. She didn't say whether that weekend had been with the girls' father. She declined to note a father on the paperwork at all.

The hell do I care about their father? Ain't I the one laying here doing all the work? Fuck a father. I see their father again, I'll make him scream like he's the one in labor.

So maybe, the nurses surmised, the best weekend of Willa's life had not happened with the twins' male parent.

They went home to the Green Lawns Bowling Club and RV Park the next day, the three Enright ladies, and Gibbs swallowed them up. It was a carnival town long past; Pastor Papa's rightful name was Hugh Atwater Gibbs the Fourth, and he'd inherited the town from his father, and his father's father, and on back to the boom days when the Gulf Coast had flourished in gold-studded citrus groves, stands of tarry pine, and fish camps where a man could buy an hour of delight or a pound of fresh-caught crab with the same currency.

His ministry was his own. None of the previous Gibbses had been men of God.

Instead, Pastor Papa denied them from the pulpit, one hand on the Bible and the other deep in ancestry's pockets. They had been the Devil's own fingers, his pappy and grand-pappy and great-grand-pappy. They'd greedily bought up the land beneath Gibbs and scraped it clean as a whistle, welcomed all manner of outcasts and felons and mother-loved runaways, twisted a hollow into the landscape like a fist socking into dough and planted it up with sin. Sin danced to the tune of tinny dulcimers and synth, sin was woven into the lacy thigh-highs of the peepshow girls, sin chivvied around the heels of the limeys as they fought one another to blood for gawking tourists' entertainment. *Sin! The Devil's path below is rose-strewn and easy, but it is sin nonetheless!*

The carnies maintained their own counsel, for wasn't it Pastor Papa who kept the lights on in Gibbs?

The town's off-season was spring and summer, when Pastor Papa's show went on the road. His white tent popped up like a canker sore, a thousand stops between the passion play in Lake Wales and parts northern, night-chilly, strange. When Pastor Papa of Gibbs, Florida rolled through a place in his tour bus of bare chrome and blazing insignia, a trickle of carnies followed. It was all very below-board. He disavowed the performers and the town and his own family, consigning them all to hellfire and flames, and then put out his hand for a wad of cash each night, coughed up from the carnival's tills. Some of the carnies were used in the ministry's morality shows, wearing red face-paint and miming the Devil; some could be counted upon to speak in tongues, handle snakes and survive a bite before pop-eyed crowds. Thus the coffers of Gibbs were refreshed, through the word of the Lord and the showmanship of Pastor Papa and, a little, the guileless pleasures of a time gone by.

At home, in the off-season, everyone else breathed a little lighter.

No one could remember which of the Enright twins had been slated for the Devil, and which for God. It came up often enough that, even had Pastor Papa not decreed it scriptural, it would've become a truism in itself. Soon enough people figured the girls' names came from their dooms, black and white, demonspawn and godsgift. Willa, who'd been present for all the particulars, merely shook her head when the girls asked who was who. They asked all the time in their younger years, for people have a terrible habit of telling small children things not even an adult can bear; they used the decree against one another. *Mom! Orca stole my sandals and broke the strap! Can the Devil have her now? Can we just give her to Him?*

No one was sure, either, how exactly God would come for His chosen, and the Devil for His.

Dice woke once, in the twins' tenth year of life, to find her sister crouched over her. Orca's hair hung down, loose rusty curls that matched Dice's own, and as Dice watched, Orca wound her hair tight about her own throat. Dice watched and watched, morbidly interested to see whether Orca's eyes would begin to bulge before blood started to seep from the roots of her hair. She fell asleep again, watching, so the outcome must've been something else entirely.

Autumn and winter were when tourists came to Florida, snowbirds no longer able to bear the icy streets of Pittsburgh and Buffalo in their truest forms, and so Pastor Papa and his disreputable retinue returned as well. The year was a wheel, Gibbs children learned, attached to God's chariot as He drove it through infinity. In the summer, the wheel turned down, exposing the world to the Devil's flames; this was why Gibbs often attained record temperatures for heat. As Tampa was inaccurately said to be the lightning strike capital of the country, Gibbs was accurately named the hottest town in the state.

Orca, something of a scientist, informed Pastor Papa during a Sunday potluck that, *actually,* Gibbs had higher-than-average temperatures because of its location inland, its flatness, and its lack of trees, *due to your grandfather bulldozing all of 'em.* She received twelve dunkings in the river for her trouble.

In winter, the wheel turned up toward God. Winter was God's season, otherwise why would He have sent His son to Earth for a December birthday? Winter belonged to Pastor Papa.

Oh, the snowy tents of the revival meetings, October through February, come one and come all! A midday luncheon on Wednesday—feed the poor, Pastor Papa believed, and the poor would feed you—and a meeting on Friday night that stretched from sundown straight up to the Devil's hour, during which the ground shook with the Spirit. New sinkholes opened oftenest on a Friday night. This, according to local doctrine, was a sign of the End Times. Baptisms were only performed in winter, cold water and air a test of the new believers' faith. Sundays were gentler, a prayer meeting in the morning where names were murmured and beseeched, and a church picnic after, and all through the week the carnies roared. This was their time. From Halloween to Valentine's Day, winter was the season of fools.

There were the usual suspects: the bearded woman who grew her extravagant mustachios in the mode of Viking warriors, braided and twined with bone beads—the flippered boy, said to be the by-blow of a local silky who'd abandoned him in disgust at birthing a son—the giant, gaunt, gray horse who loped an endless cycle in a ring too small for its plate-sized hooves, bearing an aging ballerina on its back—the strutting high-wire man, doffing his cap between splits.

There was a Ferris wheel to off-set the tent housing girls and boys, lascivious, exposed, exhausted. There was a reader of cards, and one of palms. There was a roped-off section of river with diving platforms. There were many options for good eating, all of them fried. There was another ring, with two horses in it, water-horses raised to savage each other until one dropped and blood blackened the sand. It was good betting, limerunners, better than cock-fights or dogs.

In Dice's view, it was wasteful.

Dice Enright was, in the memetic language of unkind school-children everywhere, *a horse girl*.

On the twins' fourteenth birthday, Dice gifted herself a pony, since no one was going to do the job for her. The carnival's limey wranglers had fallen asleep at the task of making sure the beasts they bought for the fights were male; more likely Caitlin and Moreau had been drunk when they'd cut their most recent deal, trading a dead limey's corpse for a fresh one, bite-ready. At any rate, a female had slipped into the pens of Gibbs, and a male had freaked for her scent, gotten loose, done what male beasts did to females. Then there was a baby. The limey wranglers shrugged over it. They knew enough to manage the fights, not raise a dad-blamed toothy baby monster, and no way could they let it stay with its mother. Nobody knew whether motherhood would soften up the limey mare, make her useless for anything but breeding. The Gibbs carnival needed a fighter, not a breeder.

For their part, the twins were eavesdroppers, as girls tend to be and doubly so for girls marked with the hands of divinity and hellfire. Dice didn't like what she heard. *How they going to kill it? It's not the baby's fault. Why they ain't just turn it loose out in Myakka?*

Orca rolled her eyes, scratching a mosquito bite in the thick wet night behind the animal tents.

To the side of Willa Enright's trailer in Green Lawns was an assortment of pathetic, would-be suburban detritus: trikes and busted kites, boards nailed to a cedar tree, a sun-bleached beach umbrella stuck into a large, spreading anthill. Empty LipSmacker tubes, sippy cups half-buried in bad soil—and a kiddie pool. Dice bought horse tranqs off one of the wormy boys who ran the Ferris wheel and spinning teacups, rather than attempt to cozen the adults who handled the carnival's animals and had reason to dish out ketamine. She moseyed up to the trailer Moreau had stuffed the baby limey into and shot the thing through one of the windows. Then she carted it home and sat it in the kiddie pool, filled to the brim with water from the RV park's communal artesian well.

"You have got to be *fucking* kidding me," Orca said when she saw the pool. She'd started cursing a lot lately, mostly *fuck* but a few *goddamns* because it made Pastor Papa's eyeballs spin, and last week, when she'd dyed her hair purple and Willa began hacking it off with scissors, *Cunt! You're a CUNT, MOM!*

Dice said nothing. The foal kept staggering upright on its spike-heel legs, then plopping down again, too woozy from the K to do anything it wanted, like bite her.

"Happy birthday," Orca said. "I guess you probably didn't get *me* anything."

The thing about limerunners, of course, was that they ate meat. Dice turned into a vegetarian, slinging any meatloaf, fried chicken, or bacon that crossed the Enright kitchen table into the pen the limey foal inhabited. She'd conned a neighbor boy into building her the pen by showing him her tits. They weren't much to look at; Enright women were bony and long like green beans that needed to be heeled-and-toed. But Nick stared and grinned like he'd never seen nipples before and then built a pen out of scrap wood and PVC stripped from the old chemical plant west of Gibbs.

Dice felt her vegetarianism was making her a better person, anyway. Chickens in Gibbs were only *free-range,* the fancy-people word, because nobody bothered cooping them. The town was half-commune as it was. Pastor Papa had some detailed, thorough doctrine on property held in kind. As Dice watched the foal gulp down fatty bacon strips and chicken nuggets and sometimes an actual chick, scooped from the main road out of Green Lawns, she felt her soul expanding. Becoming clear, like how they had to run the tap for a few minutes before the water gushed out sparkling instead of brownish. The baby limey was making her virtuous, considerate, downright wholesome.

Maybe she really was the twin who belonged to God.

Orca had long held that she herself was the twin marked by the Devil. She had a habit of searching herself, every inch of her body, for a third nipple or a strangely-shaped mole or a scar with no story behind it. She settled for a series of freckles that formed an upside-down cross on her left knee. This, she reasoned, gave her license to do whatever the goddamn hell she wanted. Nobody could tell her a thing, not her mother and not Pastor Papa, though if kids went to church in Gibbs Pastor Papa exercised his right to correct and guide them. Orca's mind was too precise for Pastor Papa's Enright decree to hold much sway, but the whole business was handy. If one of them was bad, might as well be her. It was just words, Pastor Papa's thunderings, his yammering about prophecies (*and who prophesied it? Didn't you just say your forebears were no men of God, Pastor Papa?*); it undergirded life in Gibbs but didn't require dwelling on. It had nothing to do with Orca unless she needed it for some reason.

Guess I'm the Devil's daughter, Ma. Grinning around a boy-friend's bare ass stuck in the air over her mattress.

Satan made me do it. Piously hitting 'Delete' on the video she'd taken of Dice singing to that ugly limey yearling in the backyard and posted on Instagram.

I'm possessed. Earnest, staring up at Pastor Papa after falling down in a fit of tongues and thrashing during the Friday revival.

That one lingered, and not just because her lungs burned for days afterward, consequence of her head thrust underwater, held under, pushed down, down, down. Her eyes opened in panic, the meager river current sucking at them, and faintly she'd known that she was kicking Pastor Papa's legs. Death twitch, like how people were supposed to jerk and dance when they were hanged. Sure, she'd faked the fit, yelled out a bunch of gobble-dygook and cussing, but what if it was real like Pastor Papa said?

What would it feel like, the Devil entering her body?

Orca Enright got sleep paralysis, some nights. Her mother had told her this, and Dice, and not one but several guys who had reason to know what she looked like when she slept. Her body rigid, eyes flat open and staring at the ceiling, frozen. Dice once asked what it felt like, and Orca shrugged. Not even her twin needed to know how much she liked it. It was supposed to be scary, sleep paralysis. She Googled to see if other people experienced it like her, and everyone seemed to be in agreeance about how creepy it was, how they used all their willpower to shut their eyes against the hallucinations of figures hunched on their beds, in the corners of their rooms, stretched across the ceiling.

Orca shivered over it. The visions of dark shapes, man-sized, where no man had reason to be—that was proof, right? The Devil wanted her. He'd come for her. *Come*, Orca mouthed, smirking to herself on the school bus. Her sleep paralysis never ended because she went back to sleep and woke up normal. It ended in strange ecstasy, an orgasm crashing through her while her ability to touch herself was stolen away.

'Til Satan arrived one night and drove her south, down to the Underworld like Hades stashing Persephone in his chariot, boyfriends were ok. Orca was dating her sixth boyfriend in two years on the night of Dice's big debut, so Orca figured the sis-terly thing to do would be go, Matt Lambert in tow, and watch. Clap politely. Bully Dice into downing some celebratory vodka afterward with the kids who worked the fairway, provided Dice's dumb ass didn't completely drown.

"What do you mean, they dive?" Matt said. He stared at the new high-dive, craning his zitty neck up to assess the platform, twice as broad and strong as the normal diving platform. "Your sister dives? But so what does the horse do?"

"The limerunner."

"Fuckin'…" Matt pondered. "The kinda horse they fight? I've seen 'em fight. Fuckin' nasty. Like bullfighting except they kill each other." Matt Lambert, Orca knew, had never seen a bull-fight. He probably hadn't even seen a limey fight. They were sup-posed to be one of the carnival's 18-and-above events because they were so brutal. "You can teach those motherfuckers to dive? Off a fuckin' platform?"

Maybe, Orca thought, *fuck* wasn't such a fun word after all.

"My sister's favorite movie is *Wild Hearts Can't Be Broken*," she said, knowing Matt wouldn't have a *fuckin'* clue what she was talking about. "My dear sweet sister could charm a snake into the barrel of your dad's shotgun. My sister taught her ugly little monster how to dive, because that's absolutely a smart thing for nice young ladies to do. My sister wouldn't be content with teaching a warmblood to dive, oh no, she had to go steal a limey foal and raise it like a puppy in our backyard and now, Matthew, *here they are*."

There they were.

Dice and her limerunner, whom Orca refused to call by his ridic-ulous name, were on the diving platform. Sixty feet—Orca knew this because Dice wouldn't shut up about it—and the limey poised, cool as a cat, when every other water-horse Orca'd seen or heard about was a balls-out lunatic. All teeth and venomous saliva, kill a man as soon as the scent was in its nostrils. Dice was up on his back, waving one hand like Miss America. The carnival crowd was already dying for them. Orca could tell. Every Gibbs carnie who didn't have somewhere else to be was in the stands, and every townie, and a whole slew of tourists from Tampa and Sarasota who'd heard something special was going down at the freakshow tonight.

"Mizzzzz Dice Enright," boomed the carnival's hype-man, Ted Markham, whose cue-ball head and limp mustache Orca loathed with an intensity, "and her diving limey Bubbles!"

Bubbles. Leave it to Dice to name a vicious carnivorous pony *Bubbles*.

Dice waved one more time, then patted her head. Her reddish curls were barely distinguishable from her skin; she and Orca both went brown in the summer, brown and freckles and brown and sun-streaked highlights and brown creases around Jim Beam-brown eyes. Her hair was tightly braided, and she wore a one-piece swimsuit, cut high around the shoulders and low on her hips. It was extremely un-sexy, in Orca's view, but she supposed it was made to stay on when Dice hit the water at 15 miles per hour on half a ton of predator. That would be a truly demonic wedgie.

The picture Dice and Bubbles made in the air was beautiful. Even Orca had to admit that.

They soared up, brief and sharp, the icicle edges of Dice's shoulders and the limey's split hooves silhouetted against the spotlights. Then they became bullet-shaped, Dice low on Bubbles's neck and the limey's head stretched out, his neck long and glistening. His coat was the color of old blood. They plummeted like an arrow shot from one of those monster compound bows Matt Lambert and his friends liked to take hunting, and the limey's hooves cleaved the water open like a wound in flesh. Orca saw her sister's head duck to the side as the horse raised his.

The water closed around them again, clean. Hardly disturbed.

Everyone clapped and hollered. Orca smiled. Somewhere in the crowd, she wondered if their mother was smiling too. Willa wasn't a smiler, and even though Dice was *the good daughter,* she seemed to have no great appreciation for that fact. But she had to be proud of Dice, right? It was pretty fucking cool, actually. Diving limeys. *Fucking* Dice. Nobody else would've ever thought to do it, not in a million years.

The water lay calm, seeded through with its wisp of current.

"Quooo-ite a performance, folks!" said Ted Markham, breathing into the mic. "Gibbs is proud to have Mizz Dice Enright and her diving limerunner on the roster!" More breathing, expectant and heavy, as though Ted was waiting for Dice's head to pop up out of the water, her hand to raise and wave again, her skinny arms guiding Bubbles up the bank. "Stick around and feed Bubbles a porterhouse or two for that wonderful performance!"

"Dude," Matt Lambert said. His tongue tickled Orca's ear. "Like, how the hell deep did they dive?"

They dove sixty feet through air, Dice and Bubbles. Another twenty through clear water, their intertwined shapes black and lumpy in the viewers' eyes, and the onlookers couldn't know it—applause fading, catcalls turning to murmurs and questions—but they were diving still.

At least, Dice was.

The limerunner's head appeared first, snake-like, ears pinned and eyes glowing gator-red in the falling dusk. The rest of him stood on the riverbank presently, a drowned rat of a horse, god-forsaken. Most people scattered back from the sight, but a few homegrown Florida lunkheads went up to him, tried to pet him, figured that since a little girl had ridden him, he was tame.

"Mister Hugh Gibbs, hiiiimpresario and master of ceremonies, would like to remind all patrons," said Ted Markham jauntily, "that the carnival and town of Gibbs hold no liability for death or dismemberment."

Orca took Bubbles home because she didn't know what else to do. It was *so* in her sister's wheelhouse, this bullshit (Orca walking quickly, dragging the muzzled water-horse, thinking furious thoughts because otherwise she would cry); it was so far up Dice's alley the whole concept was lodged somewhere in her major intestines. Take a stupid, hideous animal and keep it like a pet, a pet you had to feed *live chickens*. Get some idea from a movie that you could do something completely *goddamn* insane, and then actually do it. Don't bother to come back afterward, of course. Let your poor sister try to clean up after you.

Orca had never cleaned anything in her life. Her half of the room she and Dice shared was a horror story. Willa, just this side of slovenly herself, came in once a week to yell and tear down a poster or two, then retreat to the lawn chairs outside with her Coppertone.

It wasn't until Bubbles was shut up in his pen, gnawing a chicken, that Orca remembered she'd kinda left Matt Lambert hanging back at the riverside. "Whatever," she said to the limey. "He kisses like a lamprey and all he wears are stupid Gators t-shirts. He can die mad about it."

Bubbles paused in his dinner and stared at her. Blood drooled from his chops, teeth bared around the dangling chunk of hen. Then he spat it out entirely and made a keening sound, the worst sound Orca had ever heard. He kept making it as she backed away, not turning from him. It followed her into the trailer, beneath her sweat-twisted sheets, down to sleep.

It turned out that Pastor Papa took drownings very seriously.

Nobody went into the section of river running through the carnival grounds without his say-so, for water was the fluid backbone of Gibbs theology. Dice had petitioned prettily for her diving-limey show to be added to the carnival schedule, and Pastor Papa had listened, the picture of beneficence and stern love, nodding in a solemn manner every three seconds. If he knew which of the Enright twins was the godly one and which the demonic, he had never said—but Dice never sassed him at meetings, or stole rounds of pies from the Sunday potluck, and didn't go around with boys, and painted her fingernails pale pink instead of black. The general belief in Gibbs was that Pastor Papa had carried on with Willa Enright, nearly sixteen years before. No parent liked to admit it, but they all had their favorite children.

We live in the time of great signs and omens! Pastor Papa at his cedar-carved pulpit on Friday night, Willa's face closed fist-like and Orca's furious, because in Orca's view it was *extremely* tacky to use her sister as a talking point in a sermon on Friday night, of all nights, when strangers came to the ruckus and glow of the revival at Gibbs. At least he could've saved it for Sunday's quieter, members-only meeting. *Wars and rumors of war, the appearance of beasts great and strange* (what, Orca wondered sourly, did he mean the new *Jurassic Park* movie or the reticulated python that had been found in the Everglades last week), *disruption to our environment and the clouding of the minds of men!* Pastor Papa was incapable of talking without exclamation. *As God's wheel turns toward the brightest light, so sacrifices must be made!*

The wheel of God's chariot, turned heavenward during winter, would eventually revolve in place. This was the End Times, the opening of Revelation's book, the cleansing of the earth by Christ's return. Orca wasn't looking forward to it.

She squirmed as Pastor Papa went on, glaring down at her, his hands slashing like a crazed choir director for emphasis. He looked like he was doing sign language, but Orca doubted it was in any tongue area deaf people might know. His pronouncements fell on her ears dully. He had to spin what had happened to Dice, of course. Had to provide some doctrinal reason for no body floating up, in the immediate aftermath or hours later. Had to remind all present that the scions of Heaven and Hell lived among them, and that the Devil, yes, even the very Adversary Himself, Satan Son of the Morning, had claimed His prize.

It was all backward. Orca tuned out.

Meanwhile, Dice kept diving. Down and down, down down down, because if there was an original source to the springs spread like nerve bundles beneath Florida's heat-crisped surface, it was surely located in Hell. The water that cradled her changed from clear and leaf-tinged to shocking blue, then midnight blue, then black. It was cold enough just beneath the surface, and so cold far below that she knew she had died.

She wished Bubbles could've stayed with her.

Three days after Dice's little show-off moment, Orca sat on the edge of her bed and put on eyeliner. She edged each eye in thick black, upper rim and lower, and three coats of waterproof mascara. It didn't look natural in the slightest—her eyelashes, when she blinked, moved like the legs of a stick insect—but Orca wasn't interested in natural beauty.

"Ok," she said to her reflection, which didn't respond. "It's go time."

Here is what Orca Enright knew about the Devil:

He was the Father of Lies, so everything you wanted and knew you shouldn't want came from Him.

He reigned over a host of demons in Hell, and was responsible for things people called poltergeists and vampires and so forth on Earth.

He was everywhere, like yellow oak pollen in its season.

The Devil of Gibbs—Pastor Papa's rendering, in cartoony crayon colors and florid adjectives—was also the Father of Witches, which sounded metal as *hell* to Orca, and was why witches could swim, in old-timey stories. Why people wishing to test an ornery woman for witchcraft dunked her in a pond. Of course, it was Florida, and everyone could swim: thus Pastor Papa's strictness regarding the river, who went in it and why. Thus his doctrine of sinkholes, the Devil's pits opening up to trap good citizens and swallow honest folks. Thus his railings against limerunners as cloven-hoofed, fire-tongued, even as he permitted their fights at the carnival after dark. Thus the congregation's practice of water burial, totally a bundle of county code violations.

What followed Dice into the water was a tale quick on tongues before Orca even reached her destination.

Orca Enright sauntering down the main drag of Green Lawns Bowling Club and RV Park, wearing nothing but an American flag-print bikini and leading that devil horse what drowned her sister, who trotted along behind Orca meek as anything.

Orca liked her sleep paralysis so much that sometimes she tried to bring it on, the way eating a ton of Vitamin C would trigger her period when she was afraid she might be knocked up. It was easiest if she woke up in the mean small hours and then fell back to sleep before her school alarm went off. There was a space there, between night and morning, true good REM sleep and full wakefulness. She'd learned to wriggle into it, will herself into stone, freeze every bodily impulse and turn them inward until they boiled and exploded.

It was a big ol' gray area, of which Orca knew the world to be mostly composed. Pastor Papa hated gray areas. *The good Lord's word is black and white!* Then he'd beam benevolently and nod to an aged, fine-skinned African-American congregation member and again to a gingery Irish-American, to suggest that his church was one of acceptance. That he'd made a metaphor, on purpose. That, good or evil, the only requirement was knowing your place.

Orca's place was with the Devil. Her airy-fairy big-eyed sister wasn't going to steal it.

They stood at the river's edge, she and Bubbles, and though she saw people wandering over from the carnival tents to gawk, she wasn't concerned anyone would try to stop her. The limey next to her would prevent it, his big-cat teeth and can-opener hooves. She got on him, hating the slick feel of his hide beneath her legs. Nothing like the warm, vital smoothness of the carnival's other horses, which she'd pet now and then as a younger Orca, dragged along by her horse-girl sister and grimacing about it even though, ok, horses were kind of cool.

Bubbles didn't throw her, at least. He walked into the river when she kicked him.

The water was so cold that for a moment Orca wondered if Bubbles *had* kicked her. It reached into her chest like a hand gripping her heart, filled up her nostrils and punched the panic button of her brain, wormed between her legs in a way that loosened them, eased them open, tickled and cooed. Orca had about three minutes, she knew, before she'd lose consciousness underwater; another three minutes and her brain would begin to die. It was between those moments, the doorway she was looking for. If she didn't panic, if the limey didn't fight her or drag her back up to the air, they'd go down. Slip through. Swim past the gateway between the normal world of Gibbs and the darker realm of demons, bloody chambers, irresistible power.

It wasn't that the Devil had made a mistake, on the evening of Dice's diving debut. The Devil couldn't make mistakes. But they were twins, after all, alike in face and body and mannerisms. He'd just grabbed the wrong one. He'd know, as soon as Orca appeared before him, who belonged in His grasp.

They swam, she and Bubbles, plowing due south through the cave system that lay beneath the bulb of Gibbs's river. It was probably beautiful, the blue water and schools of glimmering quicksilver fish, but she kept her burning eyes open and aimed ahead. The icy flow receded around them, until it seemed that her arms and legs were dry, warm. A glance told her that she was still beneath, tiny bubbles clinging to her skin. None rose in the water before her mouth and nose. Cause for concern, but she was still moving, wasn't she? The limey still churned between her legs, his red-lined half-gills opening and closing in breath. The cave walls shrank around them, expanded, morphed into long tunnels that looked like dead ends until she reached those ends and found another tunnel. She was numb—from cold, maybe, or because she'd died and not even realized it. It was a familiar feeling, one she reached for and drew over herself like a blanket. It was that feeling of paralysis, her mind lively and pulsing inside a body now a tomb.

She would wake up again when she reached her destination.

The tunnel dipped and Bubbles's front legs sailed over the threshold, and then they were caught in a torrent, a whirlpool, the current that had bulged and subsided throughout their journey suddenly whipping into a frenzy. Orca's fingers were woven through the stringy mass that made up the limey's mane and her thighs clenched around his barrel, locked in place in a sort of rigor mortis that kept her on his back despite the wild tumble. She had a sense of plummeting over a waterfall, endlessly. Her stomach swooped and swooned, and that was familiar too: the first inklings of ecstatic sensation, blood and lust pouring through her veins, the feeling that preceded a full jolt into waking.

So another comes.

The voice reached Orca's ears faintly, as voices underwater tended to. Blurry, non-distinct, not bound by the laws of time as voices in open air. Her body arced, straining toward the source. The *source.* The mouth of Hell: that was where she'd ended up, exactly where she wanted to be.

Fair-faced, the pair of you. The voice was mirthful. That jibed with Orca's sense of the Devil. He was always laughing, Pastor Papa chided his congregants, dancing a jig as He dragged souls into His embrace.

Orca wanted the embrace.

Two theater masks of old, He continued, *see how your sister weeps? She turns from me in despair, while you... You, child—* Orca shivered inside her skin—*you descend with smiles. You run giggling to the foot of my throne. Perhaps she would smile if she saw you. Perhaps you'll cry when you see her.*

Orca, cloaked in water, had never felt her eyes more dry.

The whirlpool slowed, deposited her beside a form she knew by heart. Bubbles drifted away from Orca's legs and nudged Dice's hand. Dice's face was frozen, her mouth twisted in a silent shriek; she didn't turn to look at Orca, but her fingers flexed. They bent and settled on the limey's bat-leather ears. Orca smiled, inside her mind. There. It was all good. Dice was safe. She and her evil baby would swim back up to Gibbs (their mother would be *fine* with only one daughter, the good daughter), and Orca would stay below, in the place that had been prepared for her.

I am an eater of hearts, the voice informed her, and something twisted deep within her chest. *To truly know a person, one must consume them. Every desire comes wrapped in a different flavor, each delectable and true. Ah!* Orca observed with fresh wonder the ice-bound stillness of her body, even as sensation writhed through it. Her mind thrashed, heady, soaring on waves of pleasure. *And what a fine bouquet of nutty self-loathing, notes of popcorn grease and hidden tears. A finishing undertone of...*

His voice paused, the last words rippling through the water. Orca perched on the edge of agony.

Let us call it ambivalence.

Orca huffed, mentally. People had called her a lot of things, but *ambivalent?* Fuck that.

I am a granter of heart's wishes, He said, lovingly. *Shall I grant yours?*

"God yes," Orca said, though the words of course didn't emerge.

Beside her, Dice revolved slowly in the water. When she bobbed far enough to face Orca, her face hadn't changed. But a new awareness burned in her eyes, one of horror and painful love.

Ah-ah. There is a fight within you, child. Are you willing to roll those dice?

He'd said Dice's name, Orca reflected. Jealousy burned her throat like cheap vodka. When would He say hers?

Very well. A presence oozed into Orca's awareness on the back of the words. Far below the earth, buried underwater, the light around her grew even darker. A sensation crawled over her skin, like the air becoming electric before a storm. She burst with it, every inch of her popping against paralyzing bonds, eager to be free of the eerie liminality into which she'd forced herself. *It is most often true of humans that deepest desires are shrouded. You believe you know yours.*

Orca knew. She broadcast it to Him, imagining herself a radio tower, her pulse a wi-fi signal.

You have crossed every barrier with love in your heart, unselfish love, which is anathema to this place. This must return to the earthly world.

"What," Orca said, and this time the word did emerge. "*What?*" Muffled, the force of her shock blunted in deep water. "That isn't what I want!"

I am never wrong, child. Look to your sister. She wears your face in every regard. Look to your heart. It beats more honestly than you know.

No no no no no no no *no,* no thank you, no sirree *Bob,*

whoever the fuck Bob was. She was supposed to be here. She wanted to be here. Dice could go home, and Orca would stay, and—

Dice's hand slid from her limey's mane and laced into Orca's. Not a muscle on her skinny frame had moved otherwise. Her lips were deep, bruised blue.

Take your sister and her steed. I admit a fondness for the water-horses. They are halfway mine, two feet in the dark places and two in the light. This one—and His voice grew petty—*its teeth are blunted.*

Bubbles's teeth seemed plenty sharp to Orca.

Take your sister! The voice slipped into a crackling anger, and the current around Orca and Dice thrashed up once more. *Now, before I abandon my sweet nature. I dislike hesitation. As your people would say, half-assed-ness. Do you think to know yourself, child? Cut away those parts that buck, burn out every instance of uncertainty, before you seek my presence again.*

Orca almost believed He spat, if spitting was possible underwater.

Be grateful that these antics amuse me. On another day, in another weather, I would keep all of you for my appetizers.

Rage and shame churned in Orca's stomach. That was the force that propelled her from her paralysis. It pissed her off, that He had stolen even the nubbins of pleasure. She'd worked her ass off to get here, practically killed herself and—

Don't think to gaze back, the voice warned. The current swept Bubbles beneath Orca, and she grabbed for his mane. She clasped her arms around Dice and settled them both on the limey's back. *A glance over your shoulder, one small peek... You may see something not fit for virgin eyes.*

Was that supposed to *deter* her? God. It was like He'd never met a teenage girl. And to call her a *virgin...*

Laughter rippled out, and—against all logic—lightning struck across the cave, the bolt burying itself in black water. *Enticing, no? Search your heart once more, Orca Enright, and decide whether the feast your eyes might seek is worth your sister's life.*

His gaze, murky and vast, burned into Orca's spine as they swam upward. It was one thing to descend into Hell: all that was required, ultimately, was letting go. It turned out to be quite another to climb back out of Hell—but Orca did it, weeping invisible tears that joined the eternal current circling the cave, Dice's body slowly growing warmer against Orca's chest. That would have to be her reward, Orca reflected glumly, since it wouldn't be exactly kind to leave their mother *totally* alone. That was her reward, her sister returning to vitality, Dice's dumb bitey pony spry and mean as the day Dice had stolen him from a horse trailer, all of them back in the world of the living to function as props and doctrinal proofs for Pastor Papa.

But then, they were proof. No one had done what the Enright twins were doing right now. And no one, Orca decided with morbid satisfaction, was going to tell her *shit* when they got home.

A chuckle chased them, wrapping around Orca's bare ankles, intimate as a hand laid on her thigh. She clenched her jaw and bit her tongue and dug her heels into the limey's ribs to keep her eyes ahead. So the Devil didn't want her as she was? Orca Enright was not in the habit of taking bait and dares from men. She was flawless. *She* spurned *Him,* not the other way around.

She did not look back.

A Report of One's Honorable Death

Virginia M Mohlere

Virginia M. Mohlere was born on one solstice, and her sister was born on the other. Her chronic writing disorder stems from early childhood. She lives in the swamps of Houston and writes with a fountain pen that is extinct in the wild. Her work has been seen in Cicada, Lakeside Circus, Journal of Unlikely Coulrophobia, Strange Horizons, and Mythic Delirium, among others. This story is for tumblr user iguanamouth.

For the twenty-sixth time, the Witch of Haxe breathed blue light into her message ball and hoped.

"I have won the hoard of the Goblin of Wingmoor in fair combat. Blessings on your reign, my king, and expect this addition to your coffers by the equinox."

So far, she had killed fourteen monsters, laid eight ghosts, cured two plagues, and resolved one blight that turned out to be a bad water supply. Outright bribery was a new tactic.

"How does it work?" the Goblin of Wingmoor asked.

They were canted to one side, a loaded tray pressed against their waist.

"Give me that," the witch said. "You should've had me make the tea."

The goblin grinned, a wide line of pointy teeth.

"If I'm to be caring for myself one-handed while this shoulder heals, best to get started while there's still help within shouting distance."

Over tea, she described the message ball—a thin globe of white sapphire infused with an echo, location-bonded to herself and the palace, capable of speaking one to the other in short bursts without a time delay. The goblin touched it gingerly with two dark claws and asked technical questions of a type she hadn't thought about in years.

She was halfway through the very welcome cup of tea and about to compliment the goblin on their fine blackberry jam when the message ball glowed green.

"We thank you for your service to our kingdom and anticipate news of your honorable death."

As always, the king's voice was cold, dispassionate–that the words were identical each time made the witch wonder whether he had configured some method of using the same message, time and again. If so, it was probably a flunky receiving her reports.

As always, the message killed her appetite.

"What a curious thing," the goblin said. "Why would anyone create such an object and then use it only to be rude?"

The witch choked on her tea, and coughing made her bruised ribs smart, which prompted a couple of tears that, once started, continued in a rush while the goblin gazed at her. She couldn't read their round, granite-colored face well enough to guess their expression, but they handed her a handkerchief when she was done.

And just think, barely two candlemarks earlier, she had been beating them half to death.

"Why am I here?" she blurted.

The goblin laughed, a hissing wheeze.

"It has been long since I had interesting company, and longer still since I had a worthy adversary. You fought honorably, so it is my honor to see you away with bandaged wounds, a full belly, and clean clothes."

The witch shook her head.

"You don't seem to mind that I broke your shoulder and took your hoard."

"Do not neglect my sprained ankle and the earrings you ripped out."

"Indeed not."

The goblin shrugged their good shoulder.

"The wounds will heal. And my life is long. Before your impolite lord's heir vacates the throne, I will have amassed another hoard. But a good fight and a new conversation; those are rarities."

For conversation, at least, the witch could say the same.

The goblin lifted the message ball in one six-fingered hand. "Why does your king wish for your death but not give it himself?"

Why kept her up at night, and had for years, though she knew the answer to this part.

"They say it's bad luck to kill an honor-bound witch," she said, and the goblin nodded. "No matter how much her involvement in palace matters bothered everyone. Almost everyone."

The goblin blinked slowly, like a cat.

"Oh! Are you, then, why the king marries so late?"

"Thirty-five is not-"- she gritted, then,

"Yes," to the goblin's smile.

"Oh dear, you do carry trouble in your rucksack."

True enough.

She accepted the offer of a night's pause in exchange for another couple rounds of healing on the goblin's shoulder. After a night's sleep in a bed free of vermin and some breakfast, the sting of another refusal had faded into the background.

"I wonder whether the king's message is less direct than you assume," the goblin said when she shouldered her pack mid-morning.

What possible *less-direct* meaning could a wish for her death possibly have?

"Think on it, honored enemy," the goblin said, ensuring that she left their property with her eyes rolling.

She returned to her wandering. She'd kept a good supply of the more portable bits of the goblin's hoard, and she was past making herself tramp miserably through the muddy countryside in self-punishment, so mostly she wore herself out convincing the road to speed her along between towns and nursed her headaches afterward at slightly nicer inns.

The third town she visited, two six-days later, was festooned in pink and yellow decorations and magically reproduced drawings from which she averted her eyes.

"Royal wedding!" the innkeeper said. "This is too long coming, bless their union."

The witch smiled the smile she had carefully practiced to pull out in front of snide ministers. She wouldn't actively *curse* their union, anyhow. Even though she could.

Instead, she spent the three days of the king's wedding festival as drunk as she could maintain without blacking out, tucked into a back corner of the common room, lifting her mug and yelling vowels at every toast. Her grimace passed for enough of a smile that no one bothered her. By the time she started weeping into her beer, everyone else was too drunk to notice.

The bathhouse was full of fellow sufferers wishing for the kind release of death from their hangovers on the fourth morning. The witch sweated and hummed a tune that carried across the tubs and through the steam to quiet roiling bellies and ease sore heads. The relief of the townsfolk rebounded on her, so that she could stretch and stand straight, and possibly even face a meal before she set off.

At the fourth town, she heard rumors of trouble with livestock in the outlying houses and tramped dutifully out to see.

Wouldn't it just figure that the trouble would be an undead, stinking mess in the center of a bog?

With every step, the mud sucked at her boots, or spilled over the top to leak cold and slimy around her calves. She smelled the wight before she saw it—a stink of rot so heavy that it overcame the general stench of old mud and composting vegetation.

The wight itself might've died in the bog, its skin the same reddish tea color as the water around them. Or, she didn't want to think, the same as the king's hair. The witch gritted her teeth so hard that they creaked.

The wight opened its mouth in what was maybe meant to be a

scream but came out as a harsh whisper. It stumbled toward her, faster than she could move in the sticky mud.

A problem with dead things was that their vulnerability depended on a huge set of variables. The witch, being no necromancer and having been deprived of the royal library for three years, had to (as per usual) wing it and hope for the best. She had five spelled weapons and enough bitterness to populate a crowd. Those would have to do.

Her knife, sealed to Saint Something of Something (who could remember in the middle of a fight?), dug into the wight's chest just fine, but without effect. Meanwhile, the wight's nails raked down the witch's arm hard enough to mar leather and to draw blood at her wrist. The witch stepped back and to the side as the wight snapped its teeth toward her neck. She pulled an old trick learned from the palace master-at-arms and grabbed the wight's outstretched arm as she spun, jerking down into a crouch and a roll.

The wight's arm ripped, along with what was left of its clothing on that side. The witch came up out of the mud dripping and with the bitter taste of it in her mouth, but the wight's arm flopped at its side, not quite useless but slower than its left. The wight wheezed at her again, rushed.

Wights weren't smart, but they were extremely hard to kill, being already dead. The stubbornness that kept them in the living world was reflected in the tenacity with which they pursued whatever prey caught in the green spirit-fire that passed for eyes. Having engaged it, the witch could either kill it or contain it, otherwise it would follow her over the edge of the world.

The ensouled dagger was likewise useless.

What are you trying to achieve with this nonsense, it spat into her brain when she shoved it through the wight's abdomen.

Nothing, apparently, other than a harsh red ring around her wrist from the wight's hand.

The wight chased her through several puddles and almost caught her twice while she argued with the dagger until it would go back into its scabbard.

I'll drink your blood one day, it snarled when she finally lined it up.

"Shut up, darling, Mommy's working right now."

The dagger was so offended that it went into the scabbard without further complaint.

On one patch of dryish ground, the witch was able to turn and convince the mud to rise up around the wight's legs and solidify. It hissed and waved its arms around for several minutes while she put her hands on her thighs and caught her breath.

"You're a real pain, you know that?" the witch said once her breath evened out.

The wight wheezed and showed even more broken teeth. The mud had been willing to solidify, but wasn't too keen on fighting against the wight's struggles. It would be free any flicker now.

So. Holy knife, no good. Cursed dagger, likewise. Her demon-trapping net would only work if it were an actual demon animating the wight, but if that were the case it'd be smarter and even more dangerous. And she didn't have time to string her bow.

She hated using the little hook. Or, rather, re-magicking the little hook once she'd used it. But it was as likely to work as anything else, as long as the target was male. And in a couple of weeks she could recharge the thing with the right kind of blood.

She dug the hook out of her pack as the wight finally wriggled free of the mud. It was fast and angry, but it wasn't smart enough to have much variety in its attack pattern, and the witch had seen enough. Duck the flopping right arm, reel back from the left, and she had room to punch in under its armpit with the hook. If this didn't work, then she'd have to dismember it.

The wight paused. Its leathery, half-rotted skin made much expression impossible, but she thought she could read disgust in the lifting of its upper lip. The witch grinned and shrugged, then tugged the hook downward, ripping through the wight's chest almost to its waist. It pulled at her with its good arm, pressing against her still-healing ribs until her eyes watered.

The wight must've been a man when it was alive. Its mouth opened in another rattling exhale, and the green spirit fires went out.

With two sore arms, both bleeding at the wrist, and re-injured ribs, it took the witch far longer than she wanted to pull the wight to pieces, separate them, and burn them. By the time she was done, the sun was well below the surrounding trees, and she was too tired and hurt to make any magical aid.

She limped back to the road. Backwards lay the village she had just saved from its disgusting neighbor. Ahead lay forest – dark and unknown, but with no one who would sneer at her or ask inconvenient questions. As tired as she was, a quiet fire under a tree sounded better.

Despite the dark, and despite the way each step dragged worse than the last, the witch found fault with every moss-covered tree root. Trudging was a habit, and she indulged it, through half-lidded eyes and without a single thought in her brain. She was so zoned out that they almost missed the side road.

Three steps past the increased darkness, the witch blinked and registered what she had seen. There was magic down that trail, something sleepy, as if it hadn't been used in a long time. But it carried no flavor of malice or violence. If anything, it felt lonely.

Maybe two lonely magical beings could help one another out.

Having a potential destination put a little energy in the witch's step, despite the greater darkness of the trail, with trees bending close on either side. It wasn't far, not even a quarter of a mark, until she discovered the end of the trail and the steps of a house.

When she laid her hand on the third step, the witch learned that it was the house itself that was magic and lonely, stuck out in this forest, long abandoned.

Maybe it didn't quite actually ask her in, but it made itself clear. Inside, the house was too dark for her light to reach more than half a pace around her, and the air moved such that she knew there were missing windows and probably holes in the roof. Still, even imperfect protection was better than a swamp or an exposed camp. This deep in the forest, the witch decided to trust this lonely old house. She unrolled her blankets in one solid-seeming corner, had a strongly worded conversation with her wounds, and cast herself into a two-days' sleep to let them heal.

Only the pressing need to rid herself of water and put some back again was enough to make the witch move through the stiffness of two days lying still on a wood floor. A wounded body with forty summers on it deserved a softer bed.

By the time she had cleared the worst of the cobwebs out of the privy with a stick and encouraged the well pulley to let go of its rust and sleepiness and allow her to haul up a bucket of water, the witch felt a little less like she creaked every time she moved. The well water was frigid but sweetly metallic. After drinking, she dunked her head in it, grunting at the cold but glad to wake up. When she thanked the well, the pulley shed even more of its rusty coating.

The house was so glad to have a visitor that it felt like an embrace walking from room to room. Only one front room, furnished with a long table and hooks suspended from the ceiling like a stillroom, was in bad shape, owing to a window being open and stuck. The floor was strewn with leaves and pine needles, and various creatures had obviously come in to look around and knock down bottles of herbs and bark.

The witch found candle stubs in one of the table drawers and used one to rub the window frame. Between that and some flattery to its craftmanship, the wood consented to remember its former self, pores drawing in until the witch could lower the window shut. By the time she finished picking through the debris for still-intact bottles and sweeping the rest of the trash onto the porch, the witch could feel the house nearly thrumming with a question, and the front door trembled with the house's urge to slam it shut.

"You're very good," she said with one hand on the wall.

In the small back bedroom she found the skeleton of a cat curled up on the end of the bed, and under the quilt, a small pile of yellowish, brimstone-scented powder that was the telltale sign of a dead witch. So there was the house's mystery solved.

She returned to the still room – or, more likely, spell room – for one of the small boxes on the floor, emptied it, and carried it to the bedroom.

"Just a little longer," she said to the cat's bones. "Stick together for me, will you? And then we'll get you where you need to go."

She gathered the bones as gently as she could in her hands, and they cooperated, drooping like a living cat would, but hanging together long enough for her to set them in the box in the same curled-up shape. She bundled up the sheet – a shame to lose an entire sheet, but it would be rude if she left behind any of the dead witch. She piled the sheet on top of the bones and set the box in the stillroom, in the sun.

Whatever had happened to the witch had been quiet. There were still dried-up strings of onions and garlic braids hanging in the kitchen, and the wood pile in the back, if modest, was undisturbed. The witch passed a pleasant day, idly straightening dusty objects, nibbling at the food from her pack, and napping.

The honor that bound her was to solve magical problems. As she lay on her back on the front porch, head pillowed on her rolled-up blanket while the treetops swung back and forth, singing of wind and the dusk to come, she built the puzzle in her mind: twenty-six identical messages, the ache in her ribs and arms from her still-healing wounds. Broadwing Moor, and her "honored enemy" (still a thing to smile over) four days of magical walking away if she went in a straight line, and that little village half a day's walk. The capital city as far away as she could get and still be inside the border. This lonely house, half-alive with all the years of magic done inside it.

Witches' houses went bad, if left empty too long. Already this house had been lonely enough to throb on the forest road, enough to tug at the heart of a traveler, if not yet ready to eat one. If she weren't going to stay, solving the problem meant she'd have to burn it. This eager little house, tucked up under the trees, wanting only to have an occupant.

Her vow bound her to rid the kingdom of magical threats. Did that vow stretch so far as one semi-aware house?

While there was still light in the sky, the witch rolled to her feet, grunting only once with the pain of it, and made a closer exploration. In the stillroom, she found a set of simply-bound notebooks safe inside a cabinet. The dead witch hadn't been particularly educated or bright, but she had been meticulous, with a talent for drawing plants true to life. Her lifelong records of local plant life and the successes of various spells would make for years of winter reading and experimentation. The witch missed the royal library with a visceral pang, but this...Oh, the robed and wigged men at the palace would laugh at it, but here was one witch's personal lifetime of study, cut off before it was completed.

In the kitchen, crocks of preserved vegetables crowded one cabinet, and bottles of homemade wine another. She took a bottle labeled "Blackberry Wine" in the dead witch's clumsy hand to the fireplace in the front room. She stuck her head up into the flue, knocked out the old birds' nest, and laid a fire from the wood pile out back. She placed the sheet on top of the logs, and the cat bones on top of that, then sprinkled the lot with a bit of the wine and drank deeply. The wine was as sweet as jam, but with a strong kick that promised a good burning.

When the room was fully dark, the witch spoke to the logs in front of her of the sun and heat until they smoldered, then flamed. The scent of resin, blackberries, and sulfur rolled out toward her with the heat while she talked about rest, endings, quiet – the usual prayer for a witch to let go of the world and move to the next one without taking any last sacrifices with her.

The sheet shifted as it burned.

"It won't get lost," the witch said. "I'll take care of your work."

So she was stuck now–her honor would require her to at least care for the notebooks with her life.

A vague face formed in the smoke, elderly and frowning.

"I promise," the witch said. "I see where you were going. I know it's important. I'll keep trying."

The face shifted, as if in a nod, and dissipated as the sheet fell to ash. She felt the dead witch's spirit briefly, stubborn and strong, but tired, and then it was gone.

The cat bones shifted on top of the logs, but instead of tumbling apart, they contracted, then stretched, just like a living cat. The witch sat up straighter as a four-footed shape expanded past the limits of the bones, shimmering in the colors of fire. The bones collapsed, leaving the fiery cat shape behind.

The fire-cat arched its back, then stretched its paws in front, slightly out of the fire.

"Oh, kitty," the witch said. "Don't you want to go? It's okay to go."

The fire-cat blinked orange eyes.

"Kitty," the witch said, "it's all right. I would go, if I were you."

The cat flicked its tail and blinked again in clear ghost-cat disgust. It stepped out of the fire, delicate as a whisper, and with the last of the warmth it had used to make itself, rubbed its face against her outstretched hand, then faded.

The witch slumped, breathing past the lump in her throat. She could feel the ghost-cat sitting next to her – a mental impression of feline patience, tail wrapped demurely over paws. The cat might be patient, but the house rattled around her. Without even the remains of its former master, the house would certainly go bad now, if she chose to simply take the notebooks and leave.

A cold, unseen head bumped her knee.

"Oof," the witch said. "All right. We'll see how it goes."

Her vow might not accept this arrangement. After a week, a month, a year, it might propel her toward more monsters.

A chill wound sunwise around one ankle, widdershins around the other. The witch laughed.

Or, this might be enough, drafty and dusty as it was. What had the past three years brought her? Mud, exhaustion, and the kinds of wounds that let her foretell the weather without even asking the trees. Here, anyway, was a place to land.

She dug the message ball out of her pack and carried it to the dark little larder, hearing footsteps behind her. She breathed on the glass, and watched it glow blue.

"I inform his majesty of my honorable death," she said, not even bothering to make herself sound on the edge of expiration. "May his reign flourish in my absence."

She wiped the one teardrop off the glass with her sleeve and tucked the ball up in the back of the topmost shelf. She didn't need to hear the response again. Her word was her honor: as far as the palace was concerned now, she was dead.

On the porch, she sketched her heart's name with her thumb onto the lintel of the front door and felt the house settle. Wind might knock shingles off the roof, and nothing would get her firewood but the labor of her two hands, but no magical thing could enter the house now without her invitation. The house had its task.

The witch brought one of the old notebooks in front of the fire, with an old, greasy pencil from the stillroom. She had lists to make, of everything she needed to make the house hers and comfortable. All the things that would make it possible to stay.

Flower, Feather, Hare and Snow

Nadia Attia

Nadia Attia is a London-based journalist and Film/TV script reader, who also works as an Editor and Copywriter. She's currently writing her third novel, a folk-horror tinged rural road trip, while continuing to build a gothic short story collection.

The mountain held magic for anyone who looked upon it: 'come closer' it said, 'come run at me; I'll catch you and throw you high up into the sky like a gleeful child.' Its dangerous beauty appealed to that human instinct to explore and conquer, that strange need to gaze down upon the rest of existence. Whether it was to feel superior to all the other creatures on Earth or to remind them how insignificant they were, Liath couldn't tell. Either way, it was time to count the bodies.

She'd never wanted for anything; nature always provided, and her humble tools excelled where the torches, tents, crampons and compasses of men had failed. People often blamed their tools – they didn't remember the old ways and couldn't read the signs. Liath knew when a storm was coming, thought it was obvious, but not to the walkers, they always seemed taken by surprise, blinded by the whorls of snow or rain. Their curses and cries rode the back of the wind.

She shook beads of heather from her silver cloak and slipped it over her head. It could catch a glimmer in the murkiest of dawns, in a snow shower it reflected each crystal as it spun and danced, and in full sun it was dazzling to behold. To those below she must have seemed a beacon, or a will-o'-the-wisp stalking the slopes and plateaus after a bitter and lonely night. Some called her Nan, but most knew her as Liath, the grey one, on account of the cloak, she supposed, but also her hair, which tumbled down her back like soft boulders. It had been mud-brown once, but time had changed her, and time was the only thing in the whole of existence that she truly feared.

The morning was as peaceful as the night had been wild – not that the average eye would be able to tell: the snow hushed the frozen streams beneath its belly, and masked the scarps and gullies, making all things equal. It betrayed the birds and hares, though, and Liath followed the paw prints to the first site, where she found a mound and a lump that had no business being there. She knew in this spot the frozen mass would be easy to miss, the sun would take too long to thaw it and the arctic winds would barely stir it, so yet again it was up to her to clean up the messes that people left behind. Liath tucked her hair behind her ears and knelt down to dig, hardened to the cold after all these years. Her slender fingers scritched and scuttled until they'd uncovered the head and torso of a shepherd who had taken shelter in the overhang. His faithful collie lay curled up by his feet. She looked a long while at the young man and felt nothing; she wasn't moved by the tightness of his pale skin, nor his lavender lips or smooth eyelids, frosted shut in a forever sleep. She mourned the dog, however, knowing that it could have found its way – had the strength to run but chose to stay. Liath entwined a single star-flower around its collar and piled stones up next to the two of them, a cairn to mark the place so that they'd be found and removed by the walkers, skiers and climbers who never stayed away for long.

Then she followed the hare prints a long, winding way that veered on and off the path forged by others – whoever it was had been so close and yet so far from salvation. She passed through a cloud, or rather, a cloud passed through her, and when she emerged she was surprised to find a little gloved hand pressed into hers and a young face staring up at her.

The boy tugged at Liath, puffed out his ruddy cheeks. "My dad, he's hurt."

She nodded and he led her quickly away, surefooted and quiet as only the dead can be. If only they'd been so sure the day before, his feet might have found the bothy that lay in wait just over the ridge.

They cut through a straggle of gorse and on the other side the boy paused. "I left him here, to get help," he said, his head switching left to right. "He was right here!"

Liath placed her hand on the boy's shoulder and gently turned him towards the hare. It sat watching them with round glassy eyes, silken ears pricked. At its feet is where Liath began to dig. As she chipped away at the white crust, the boy pressed closer and peered into the hole she was making.

"Please hurry!" His pinched voice sounded more like the gargle of a ptarmigan, and this stirred her a little, she had to admit.

Inside the hole lay father and son, unmoving bundles of blue and orange. The boy was on all fours, arms outstretched as he'd tried to claw himself out, but the man must have given up long before.

"Dad?"

When Liath spoke some said it sounded like moss-covered pebbles knocking together, others compared it to the winnowing of ice from rock. "The man is gone," she said, "as are you."

The boy looked at the other boy, the shell of himself, and then up again at Liath. His eyes flickered with confusion, then realisation. "But it didn't hurt... I didn't feel anything. I thought dying hurt!"

"It's just a change from one thing to the next. Sometimes it hurts, often it is painless and simple." Liath reached over to the outstretched body and threaded a single feather into the boy's hair, and as she did so his ghost loosened and fell like a new dusting of snow.

She stacked the stones to mark the place, drew her up hood and left.

By now the mountain was blushing in the sun and she knew that in a few days the melt would wash away the outlines of the bodies and sweep their tears into the lochs, making the land fresh and clean again. At least for a while. Liath finished her rounds on the very summit that had lured so many to their end, and gazed out at the world flowing from the hem of her skirt. It intrigued her still: she marvelled at how it had been broken and remoulded many times over, brutally gouged by the elements – yet to her each new face looked as beautiful as the last. Then Liath's thoughts took a darker turn as she wondered how long would it be until she weakened and crumbled like that boy who had held her hand. Would she become nothing more than a pile of dust? Something shuddered in her chest. She worried, then, that she might be getting soft like the wayfarers who crawled up and down her slopes – looking for what, she did not know...

Seeing Utopia

Lisa Fox

Lisa Fox is a pharmaceutical market researcher by day and fiction writer by night. She enjoys crafting short stories and short screenplays across genres, but her passion is for Sci-Fi/Drama hybrids. She thrives on the thrill of creating something out of nothing, in transforming life's 'what ifs' to prose that flashes a mirror on the human condition. As a writer, nothing makes her happier than having readers say that her work made them feel something or look at the world in a different way.

Queen Aclara had lost track of how many days she'd languished in the dungeon. She knew the number of stones on the walls and ceiling of her cell. She'd counted the number of iron bars behind which she wasted away, even took comfort in tallying the links of the chains that bound her. But the days eluded her. They'd relented to one endless night of suffering, punctuated only by the howls of anguish echoed in the halls of the castle above and the Sorcerer King's demonic laughter.

She couldn't remember the last time her voice had succumbed to her own screaming as she tried to quash the sounds of the pain she had blindly welcomed into her kingdom. Her cries reminded her she was still alive, still human; but in the silence when she lay with cold stone pressed against her cheek, she wondered if Death had crept into her cell to take her next.

Just as Death had taken her kingdom when she'd pledged herself to Elwin of Erylo. His whispered promises had fallen sweet, like rose petals, and she promised her life and love and the kingdom of Videre to his care. But the skies had changed the moment they'd said their vows, yielding to a darkness that consumed the stars. Aclara hadn't realized she'd kissed death until their lips parted and she tasted blood. Thunder boomed, knocking her to the ground as he peeled back his mask, revealing a demon camouflaged under the guise of a nobleman with a smile as bright as the River Moon rising over azure waters.

No, Aclara had not seen through evil's clever disguise. Wedding bells blunted the death knell that resounded across the kingdom, over the people and land she loved.

And he took everything.

Aclara pulled her legs to her chest to quiet the pangs that churned her gut, the need for water and food overpowered only by a yearning for her people's freedom. In the darkness, she felt something brush against her leg and pulled her body in tighter, knowing the rats shared her hunger.

She thought she heard a voice. Faint. *'Hello?'*

Aclara teetered on a shaky precipice, hovering between life and death. *Perhaps I am dreaming? Hallucinating?* A man materialized beside her, morphed from the shadows, flesh and blood with large, soft hands. He released her chains and lifted her from the floor, cradling her like a child. She tried to speak but could only choke out a raspy cough.

The man's image flickered as he carried her up the steps leading her from hell. His form dissolved in the shadows. Aclara lay, limp, in his invisible embrace, as if she were floating back up to the living.

He pushed open the door, and Aclara gulped in the night air. It tasted of fire and ash, smelling not of the yensi flower whose vines climbed over the castle walls, but of smoldering wood and pulverized stone.

She squinted in the twilight and held tight to the man's vest as a crowd cheered around her. Her invisible savior held tight to her waist as he lowered her to the ground, her bare toes nestling into ash. She opened her eyes to the cacophony, but saw no one, save for the Sorcerer King, whose head was perched on a stake, his green eyes as wide and menacing in death as they were in life.

The man who'd saved her flickered back into view; his face round, adorned by a graying beard. He had kind brown eyes. With a flick of his hand, he produced a ladle of water and as Aclara drank, he introduced himself as Mollo, Wizard of the Hamlet Andle.

Cheers again erupted in the empty courtyard. Aclara was confused.

A hundred patches of dust shimmered around her. The golden boots of as many peasant soldiers materialized, followed by their sweaty, exhausted bodies. They knelt before her.

Aclara smiled weakly. The Sorcerer King's pride blinded him; he never would have suspected an army of commoners to rise against him.

She gestured toward the severed head glaring at them from the stake. Mollo followed Aclara's eyes.

"We must burn it," he said. "Spread the ashes deep in the sea so this evil never returns."

Aclara nodded. Mollo murmured an incantation unintelligible to the Queen and raised his hands. Blue flame engulfed the head in a demonic halo. Amid the conflagration, the Sorcerer King's eyes glowed emerald green. Aclara stared deep, silently willing those eyes to close one final time.

She let go of Mollo's grasp and walked forward, her steps tentative as a baby dragon in the snow.

"Your Grace?"

But Aclara didn't hear Mollo above the fear that reduced his voice to a whisper. She didn't see anything but those eyes that hovered in the inferno, pulling her closer. Aclara reached toward the radiance emanating from those eyes, her fingertips smarting as her hand approached the flame.

And with a burst of light, the skull of the Sorcerer King imploded, leaving a swirling plume of black ash that moved above them as if it were breathing. Sucked inward by a violent centripetal force, the remains of the Sorcerer King contracted into a tight bullet that fired directly into Aclara's wide-open gaze.

***

Gerard tapped the tip of his cane against the Queen's chamber. The cane was crafted from the wood of the Degal tree, bent and knobby yet sturdy as steel – just like Gerard himself. His joints ached from the strain of a century's use, but as Royal Valet, he was committed to the needs of the rulers he served. Never was a request made nor a challenge presented that Gerard did not oblige – even for the Sorcerer King, who saw service and servitude as being one in the same. Gerard remained true to task even as the King spat on him, cursed and kicked him. His body and spirit ached; each movement a reminder of his years. But Gerard was a survivor, and would carry on.

It had been a fortnight since the Sorcerer King's fall, yet the kingdom still felt his presence in the mantle of despair that lay upon it. Scouts described villages quiet as the grave, as if entire communities held their collective breath against evil that lingered in the air. Commoners holed up in damaged homes, peering through windows as broken as their souls. Nobles kept their bridges drawn; wizards and witches stayed close to their oracles, waiting for a signal of changing winds. And at night, the cries of hungry children harmonized with the distant howls of wolves.

The Queen had not left her chamber.

Gerard tapped louder. Beyond the thick oak, he heard shuffling and finally, a click, as the door cracked open.

"Gerard?" Aclara stretched her arm through the opening, grasping until her hand touched Gerard's shoulder.

"Dear child." He slid his arm through hers, leading her back in to her quarters. She stared ahead, eyes glowing opaque white, as Gerard brought her to a settee near the window. He frowned as they walked past the royal family's coat of arms – a purple dragon shimmering atop a river of gold – and rich tapestries depicting the verdant orchards of the South, knowing that Aclara would only see them again in her dreams. And the Queen's own paintings: sunrise and sunset over the Sea of Delas, rainstorms and rainbows, and faces – the faces of the people, the youthful, the aged, the elated and downtrodden. The kingdom she beheld in a way no other ever had.

"Have you rested?" Gerard squeezed her hand. Her slumped shoulders, slow breaths, and pallor saddened him. Though she was his Queen, Gerard regarded Aclara as he would a niece, perhaps even a daughter. He silently cursed the fates.

"How can I rest?" She lowered her head, red curls a veil. "My kingdom bleeds and I've no way to stop it."

"Indeed, the pain persists." He frowned. "But your kingdom is free."

"Freedom does not heal the wounds that brutality leaves." Aclara rubbed her wrist, the fresh purple bruise a reminder of her captivity. "I can't see the way back, Gerard. Nor the way forward."

"Your love for your people will be your beacon." Gerard leaned on his cane, kneeling beside her.

"The Sorcerer King took more than just my sight." She shook her head. "What is a leader without a vision? One cannot build a castle with a single stone. Or fill an ocean with just one raindrop."

Gerard patted the Queen's hand. He'd lived long enough to know that when hope was needed, hope would arise. "You need not carry this burden alone. Sometimes we see more clearly through the eyes of others."

***

Myth hummed as she sat at her work table in a cottage deep in the Dorwol Woods. She'd first heard the tune upon the kingdom's liberation, when the twitter birds proclaimed the good news, and it stayed with her. Waving her wand in harmony with the song, the silken threads hovering above her danced under her spell, weaving themselves into a shining cape. She was surrounded by multi-colored tapestries, bejeweled cloaks, and hats of various fabrics and sizes. Rows of shelves spanned floor to ceiling, holding dozens of identically-styled shimmering gold boots that intermittently blinked in and out of sight.

"Can you believe it? The Queen herself, calling upon the likes of us. Papa would be so proud."

Dust motes coalesced, as if magnetized, and Myth's twin sister Janin materialized on the empty bench across from her. Though they had shared the womb, Myth and Janin could not be more different. Janin was svelte, with a shock of midnight blue hair cropped close to her scalp, the color matching the steel in her eyes. Myth was plump. Bright yellow, green, and orange hues danced within her amber eyes; her pink hair, soft as a fairy's wing, grazed the floor.

Ankles crossed, Janin rested her feet on the table. She wore the same golden boots that lined the shelves.

Myth pursed her lips and sighed. "How many times did Papa tell you to keep your boots off the table?" *A witch's table is a sacred space.*

She brought her wand down. The unfinished cape fell across Janin's legs, but she didn't budge.

"Father was a better wizard than he was a soldier," Janin said. "But, without his sacrifice, we'd still be under the rule of King Crazy."

Myth frowned. She didn't like to think about how her Papa died, how there was nothing left of him to bury. Instead, she preferred to remember how he lived. "When I was a little girl, Papa told me stories of the Great Oracles. He said they'd predicted I was destined for great things."

Janin snorted. "He only said that so you'd stop feeling sorry for yourself every time I beat you in Cauldronball."

"I never felt sorry for myself." Myth shook her head. "Besides, you didn't *always* win."

"Believe what you'd like." Janin slid her feet off the table and stood, stretching. "The Queen's entreaty is logical. Of course, she would consult us." She gestured toward the footwear on the shelves. "The army never would have infiltrated the castle without the Cloaking Boots I designed."

Myth cleared her throat. "You mean, the boots *we* designed. You and me." Her voice came out in a squeak. When Myth wasn't standing in her sister's shadow, Janin often seemed to find a way to make a shadow find her. And Myth much preferred the light.

"I should have been there," Janin said. She'd had ambitions to lead the charge against the Sorcerer King, but Papa had forbidden it, casting a sleep spell over his daughter until the siege was complete. As Janin awoke and the fog lifted, Myth saw in her sister's face a pain that seemed sharper than a thousand thorns. Though they never spoke of it, Myth wasn't certain if Janin had been more upset about her father's death, or that someone beside herself had sealed the King's fate.

Myth lifted the unfinished cloak from the table and raised it, fabric spinning, threads weaving at her whim. "It's up to us to create a new fashion for the Queen, to lead us back to brighter days." Myth threw a splash of pink on the garment; it sparkled in the dim light. "Dear sister, our design will color the destiny of all of Videre!"

Janin sat on the bench, her features pinched with thought. She thrummed her fingers on the table. "It should be sturdy. Tailored for the Queen's long-term aspirations."

"Something beautiful." Myth sighed. The gold and pink hues of the fabric hovered above them like sunrise. "Something whimsical."

"Practical," Janin said. "Probing. Sleek, yet authoritative. An accessory of wisdom and strength. To bolster the crown."

"Stylish, yet inconspicuous." Myth ran her fingers through her hair and smiled. "An accessory of beauty and grace. A complement to the crown."

The two witches sat upright. The spinning cloak floated across the room toward an empty shelf, slinking away from the tension brewing beneath it.

"True vision entails seeing the world for what it is." Janin folded her hands and leaned in toward her sister. "Our design will help the Queen find truth."

Myth shook her head. "To rebuild the kingdom, the Queen needs to see its rebirth. Its possibilities."

Janin pushed herself back from the table, scowling. "Possibility is what plunged our Queen, and our kingdom, into despair. It is time to look deep into the heart of the darkness, to prevent it from ever rising again."

Myth stood, glaring up at her sister who stood a head taller than she. Myth levitated until they were eye to eye. "Only light can cut through the darkness."

Janin folded her arms across her chest. Myth mimicked her sister's body language; together they were a mirror image of stubbornness.

"And I'm sure that if Elwin of Erylo had only felt the light of Aclara's love, they would have lived happily ever after." Janin smirked. "You are soft, dear sister. And your magic suffers for it."

Myth felt her ruddy cheeks flare. "And you are as cold and unyielding as a... as a..."

"Good luck with your design," Janin said. Her form flickered, then dissipated, leaving Myth alone.

Myth floated down and settled back in to the bench. The unfinished cloak glided toward her, wrapping her in a hug.

***

Queen Aclara listened to the murmuring crowd that had gathered in the courtyard. She wiped sweat from her brow as the heat of the summer sun beat down. With the King gone, daylight had finally ventured out like a child emerging from her hiding place. Aclara's time in the dungeon had given her an appreciation for the warmth she had long taken for granted.

"How many are there, Gerard?"

"Maybe two hundred, your Grace. Mostly peasants. Some nobles, few wizards." He squeezed her hand. "It's a start."

"And the two witches? Have they arrived?"

"They have. Each with her own design. Apparently, there were creative differences."

"Sisters." Aclara smiled. "It's to be expected."

"And their quarrel is to our advantage." Gerard laughed. "Sometimes a friendly competition is all you need to bring a kingdom back together."

***

Myth raised her hand to her eyes as she looked skyward. Purple and gold banners – the Queen's colors – rustled in the breeze. She felt a nagging tickle in her stomach as the Queen's valet led her and Janin, whom she hadn't seen in weeks, to a large platform. Myth grasped tight to the pink satin sack that held her design; Janin carried one similar in dark blue.

Myth hated the way they'd left things and was anxious to see Janin's creation. But based on Janin's stony expression, rigid as a castle gargoyle, she suspected that her sister didn't share the same feeling of goodwill.

The crowd quieted as Queen Aclara stepped forward to address them. It was her first public appearance since her captivity, and the first time Myth had ever seen her in person. Though slight in stature, her movements betrayed a heaviness that only tragedy, and uncertainty, bring. Nonetheless, Myth thought that Aclara was the most beautiful woman she'd ever seen.

"My loyal subjects," the Queen boomed, her voice belying her mousy exterior, "today we celebrate our lives and our freedom."

Aclara's subjects cheered tentatively, as if they feared excessive joy would conjure the evil that had enslaved them all.

The Queen continued. "Standing before you are two witches whose vision, expertise in the art of magical design, and unparalleled bravery helped to break the chains that bound us under the Sorcerer King's reign."

Myth smiled. She had never considered herself brave. Father was brave. Janin was brave. But she? Optimistic, perhaps. But not brave. She glanced again at her sister, who nodded, solemnly.

"The evil that impaired me under the guise of love is irreparable, my blindness his final act intended to break our kingdom." The Queen paused and drew in a deep breath. "But we will not be broken."

Myth stood close enough to see that Aclara's jaw quivered. Before the Sorcerer King had seduced her, the Queen had been an artist, a poet, and the type of ruler who governed like a master chess player. Myth blinked back hot tears as she realized all that the King had taken, the shell left behind, and how difficult it must have been for her to stand before them today.

"I will never regain my sight. But today, Myth and Janin will share the magic of their vision. And the one I deem most worthy will stand by my side as Royal Seer of the Kingdom of Videre."

Myth's eyes widened. She watched Janin shift her weight, a twitch in her cheek the only hint of her sister's surprise.

***

JANIN scowled, standing on the hillside outside the castle walls. The crowd had followed through the gates to witness the first challenge, and though she was secretly pleased with her odds at becoming the Royal Seer, she felt like a pawn. Aside from a proper match of Cauldronball, Janin didn't much like games. These festivities were far better suited for her sister, who enjoyed this type of pomp and circumstance. Janin just wanted to get on with things.

Gerard hobbled forward, supported by a cane bearing the pewter head of a dragon on its handle. His back was crooked and arched; time etched into his skin with wrinkles as deep as the bark of the Dorwol tree. "Your first task will demonstrate your vision of the life force."

Gerard nodded toward Janin. "Fidelis the dragon, Queen Aclara's lifelong companion."

Guess I'm leading this jester-fest, she thought.

The purple dragon snored beneath a willow bush. He wasn't much bigger than the shrubbery. Faint puffs of smoke wafted from his nostrils. His scales were molting, his snout graying, and a large black bruise the size of a watermelon blemished his neck.

"People of Videre," Janin said, raising her voice loud as a trumpeter's call, "behold the Shade of Perlustrate." She retrieved a sleek black satin beret, placed it on her head, and pulled down a dark shade, like a knight's mask save for its translucence. "True vision entails seeing beyond the surface. We need to delve into the depths of our humanity to unmask our shortcomings. Eradicate our weaknesses."

The shade flashed and midnight blue granules beaded on the mask. They detached, darting in the air above the crowd as if in pursuit of an invisible foe. They flew toward the dragon's chest and disappeared, burrowing into his skin. He emitted a low groan, breath unsteady, as he exhaled.

Brows furrowed, Janin squinted through the shade and observed a green aura around the dragon, rising like a poison mist. As she probed deeper, she felt the weakening pulse of his turquoise veins, she watched the blood trickling through them like a stream about to run dry. A parasite the size of a tortoise, with legs spindly like a spider's, squeezed his heart. She lowered her chin and removed the apparatus, her hairline moist with sweat.

"Good Witch, what did you see?" Queen Aclara brought her hands together, as if in prayer.

Janin glanced at the waiting crowd, and at her sister whose gaze was fixed on Fidelis. She shook her head.

"I'm sorry, your Grace. His heart will not beat for much longer."

The crowd mumbled disapproval. This was not the vision they sought, nor the news they had hoped for. The Queen turned away.

Gerard motioned toward Myth, who had been trying to capture Janin's attention since their arrival at the castle. Though Janin had not welcomed her sister's emotional distractions, she didn't want Myth to paint herself the fool. With a sharp nod, Janin attempted to warn Myth to control her exuberance.

Janin held her breath as Myth stepped forward. "My fellow citizens," she said, her voice quavering.

"Louder!" someone shouted.

Myth cleared her throat and raised her chin. "I am honored to present to you The Spectacles of Hope."

She wiggled her chubby fingers over the bag's opening. Rose-colored glasses, adorned with rubies and quartz stones, floated from the sack and hovered above Myth's head.

"True vision lies in seeing the potential around us. Viewing the world for what it can be."

The jewels glowed, a prism of color exploding from their core. The glasses floated down, feather soft, until they rested on Myth's smiling face. The gemstones glowed, bringing out the color in Myth's cheeks. She moved closer to the dragon, regarding it with wide eyes. Myth frowned, wringing her hands.

"I'm afraid my sister is correct," she said. "Your Grace, this dragon is gravely ill."

She approached the Queen, laying a hand on her shoulder.

"But I do see a happy creature, spending his last days with joy," Myth said. "It may be past, it may be future, it may be a dream, but Fidelis sees himself in a meadow of adaflowers surrounded by children who tickle his belly." She gestured toward the dragon and smiled. "Did you know that dragons can giggle?"

The Queen grasped Myth's hand.

"You have given this dragon a very happy life," Myth said.

"Thank you," the Queen whispered.

Janin scowled. From anyone other than her sister, Janin would have thought the vision contrived, a testament to that which the Queen and her people wanted to hear. But Myth was different.

***

Myth strode toward the crumbling village of Yobho for their next task: to convey their vision of the kingdom. The shuffling of the crowd's feet behind her nearly drowned out her own breaths.

Closest to the castle, Yobho had suffered the worst of the Sorcerer King's siege. Myth prayed to the deities that her magic was strong enough to cut through the gray cloud that still hovered over this hamlet.

Myth brought the glasses to her face. The world glowed around her, her body draped in a pink halo. Like a specter, she moved from the crowd and looked outward. The gray swath dissipated, revealing above a cloudless, cerulean sky. Rubble wriggled from the ground, filling the cracks of damaged buildings until the walls were smooth, transfigured from stone to marble, a kaleidoscope-burst of color painting each in a shimmering mosaic. Vines rose and flourished in the village center, bearing fruit three times the normal size. Children splashed in the clean water flowing from a fountain of unblemished porcelain.

And in the forest beyond, dead evergreens righted themselves. A flock of singing twitter birds swooped by in symmetry. Well-groomed coyotes sat watching, swaying in the delight of their song.

Myth turned toward the crowd, breathless.

"Ours is a kingdom of infinite beauty," she said. "Magician, noble, and commoner eat the fruit from the same lush vine. Dragon and dog sleep side by side and bird and coyote are friends. With unity and love, we can be whole again."

Gerard pushed through the crowd with Janin by his side. Myth struggled to read her sister's countenance. The rigidness of Janin's jaw, the thin line of her mouth, her perfect posture –all classic Janin. But there was a heaviness in her eyes that rivaled all the stones in the castle walls.

Once again, Janin pulled down her visor. The granules formed and flew into the village and the forest beyond.

"Buildings on the verge of collapse. A patch of dirt in the village square, overgrown with weeds of poison. Starving animals, starving birds seeking sustenance. All potential predators. Dangers everywhere."

Janin removed her visor and rested it on her hip. "Your Grace, it will take an army - carpenters, masons, botanists, experts in animal husbandry, and a visible police presence to rebuild." She looked toward Myth. "This village needs more than love."

Myth hung her head. Once again, Janin cast a shadow. Her sister clearly didn't understand.

***

Queen Aclara took both Myth and Janin by the hand. Though she had never seen either with her own eyes, she painted each in her mind, just as she had captured her people in the care of her brushstrokes in a time that seemed so long ago.

In her imaginings, Myth was the girl with a perpetual smile, the best friend who ran beside you, never overpowering even as your own gait slowed. She transformed dandelions to roses, tree bark to chocolate, always laughing. Warmth emanated from her like the summer sun on the beaches of Matee. And Janin, she was sharp. Smart. She ran ahead, not to win, but to push the rocks aside and warn you of errant roots rising from the forest floor. From her, Aclara felt the cool, swirling breeze that signaled the start of winter. She was the rise of the moon, the setting of the sun, steadfast as the ancient Dorwal trees.

Janin's vision validated Aclara's suspicions about Fidelis; she knew the dragon was dying, but Myth's assurances offered her comfort. Royal scouts affirmed the persistent dangers wrought by the damage to the villages that Janin identified; and Myth's vision provided perspective on how she, as ruler, could inspire the kingdom to flourish once again.

Perhaps Gerard was right, she thought. We do see things more clearly through the eyes of others. But Aclara needed them to pass one final test – the one she had failed.

Aclara addressed the crowd. "People of Videre, this final challenge is perhaps the most important. For it is one thing to envisage life, and another to have the vision to rebuild a kingdom. But without the ability to see the true character of those around us, lives and kingdoms can be lost."

***

Janin hadn't expected the Queen to admit her failings in public; the tittering crowd and Myth's wide-eyed stare validated that others shared the same view. *So much easier to confess one's sins in darkness*, Janin thought, *like in ancient times.* The Queen trembled as she adjusted the crown that seemed too large for someone of her stature. Janin wondered which burden was heavier for Aclara to bear - the guilt of her prior mistakes, or the fear of making new ones?

"Dear Myth," the Queen called. "What is your vision as you behold your sister?"

Janin opened her mouth and just as quickly closed it, setting her jaw tight. She swallowed hard to quell the flutter rising from her stomach, and wished she had the good sense to wear her Cloaking Boots. A clean disappearance would have been more valuable than all the gold in Videre. Janin's steps were always sure; she never stumbled down any path she chose to travel. She never doubted the veracity of the looking glass. But the mirror had never talked back until today.

Myth approached, grinning. The gemstones on her glasses shimmered, reflecting the changing color of Myth's eyes. A kaleidoscope of color burst from her spectacles, bathing Janin in a rosy haze. Myth was like sunrise over a snow-covered field. Janin felt warm gooseflesh creep over her skin in a sense of calm she had never experienced before.

"I see a woman with strength I could only dream of," Myth said. "Bearing the intelligence of a kingdom within an erudite mind. A truth teller, brave enough to voice her opinion, even when her viewpoint is not favored."

Myth removed her glasses, but her glow lingered. "In my vision, the newest member of the Queen's royal counsel stands here before you."

Janin's lower lip quivered, and possibly for the first time ever, she didn't resist it. Without invitation, she donned her visor and peered back at Myth. The granules rose and darted over her sister, surrounding her in a cyclone. The black spheres burst into diamonds as the centrifuge spun around her.

"I see a woman with warmth I could only dream of." Janin's

voice cracked. "Bearing the kindness of a kingdom within a selfless heart. An artist who sees beauty all around her, whom the oracles have marked for greatness."

Janin removed her visor and cupped her sister's hands within her own.

"I am honored to stand before the Royal Seer."

***

Aclara was swept away by the crowd's cheers, unbridled as the crashing tide. The magic kindled by these two witches would light the torch that would lead Videre through these long, final hours of night to a dawn painted with gold. And though Aclara would never see the sun rising with her own eyes, she would feel it warm on her skin. She would taste the sweetness of morning, thick like the juice of the mayca fruit. Videre would be rebuilt. It would flourish. Its people would persevere.

"Faith and fact, potential and practicality - the cornerstone upon which our kingdom will be rebuilt. Myth and Janin, together your vision will help us see our utopia."

Aclara repositioned her crown. For the first time since she suffered the Sorcerer King's kiss, it rested lightly upon her. She held her head high.

The Fire Wife

Erin McNelis

E.K. McNelis has been reading fantasy
literature for most of her life. Her
favorites begin at the beginning with
Lloyd Alexander and more recently
N.K. Jemisin. She writes and reads in
Pennsylvania with a husband and two
children who think they are dragons.

The old woman who wore mimebird feathers in her hair dropped six wrist-sized sticks into the fire pit. She bent down, making of her figure a lump of rock or a far hill or a tree stump. She took metal and a rock that she had been allowed to keep and clumsily struck them together. And of course, nothing happened. *You're doing it wrong,* I thought at her. I should know. A fire wife knew better than anyone how to make a fire happen. But I couldn't tell her that.

The feather woman looked up at me, smiled a gapped smile, and shrugged, laughing a little. I couldn't tell her, but I supposed I could show her. The Odds Camp, where the saddest and lowest victims of war were kept, hardly seemed the place to hold firm the precepts of civilized society. She was my elder, yes, but if we were to eat hot food and not freeze that night, I would have to dishonor her. I was ashamed, and not even sure I would be successful. But she wouldn't be.

I picked up a few pieces of kindling at my feet and took them to the fire. I watched the anger in her face until it dissipated and became recognition of who I had been before the war. I looked around and then put a dirty finger to my lips. She sat, and I carefully took apart her fire and built a new one. By the time a few weak yellow flames were attempting to overtake the kindling, feather woman had put her arms around me, our bodies trembling with the tears each of us thought to keep secret.

Feather Woman never spoke. I don't know if she could. Silently we watched each batch of refugees with sideways looks as if we were merely curious. But as the days passed and our desperation grew like a flame fanned by a high wind, we cared less for being careful. When the gates opened and those who answered to the conqueror marched our tribespeople through those gates in mangled lines, we were the first to drop our meals or feather gathering and run to watch the newcomers. I searched every face that came through for anyone I knew. Each time there was no one, I forced a smile. That meant they had gotten away, I told myself. He was safe. But I wanted him there with me, too. With his help, I thought I might actually be able to make some new, whole life out of the pieces of kindling the conqueror had left of me.

Feather Woman, I soon learned, did not wait for herself. She came with me, mirroring my emotions. One day, as I smiled my lie of a smile, she clapped her hands together like a happy child who has just seen a butterfly for the first time. I put an arm around her on the way back to our corner and squeezed.

And so in this manner, I existed, for what may have been months. We ate the meager food our captors allowed us. We built little fires. We kept to ourselves. And of course, Feather Woman collected feathers. She found them in the yards, the pathways, and snagged in the metal fence that surrounded the whole of the Odds' Camp. She wove each one into her hair slowly, hands heavy with bulbous knuckles. I watched as her hair became less hair, it seemed, and more feathers, until her head was covered with them. I smiled at Feather Woman and wondered what she called me in her head when she thought about me, if she did.

Maybe I was Once Fire Wife or Used to Have Magic or simply No Tongue.

***

The conqueror's men had come before I could build the fire large enough to cover me. I was going to save my village, but they came before I could.

The onions had sat, three to a row and three to a column, next to three heads of garlic, three acorn squash, and then the chicken, already plucked, tied and dressed with rosemary. I had smoothed out my apron, taken a deep breath, a moment of calm, and then I began.

Deep into the chopping and sautéing, Shen had filled the doorway, watching, the only sound he made the breath rattling in his nostrils. When I turned to look, the chief's oldest son met my eyes and smiled. The smile had none of the tilt or snarl of lust, unlike the other men in the tribe. They all want what they cannot have. His smile was genuine happiness to see me.

"Mistress Aruna," he said, losing the smile. *Oh, beautiful Shen,* I had thought. I had always thought. *If I weren't wed to the fire.* I had been fire wife in the chief's home for three years and had hidden my love for Shen for nearly that long. "My father wishes to see you. It is urgent. There's been a rider from the hills." The meal went half prepared. I thought about refusing, something well within my power, but curiosity was more persuasive than a demonstration of power. I wiped my hands on my apron before removing it and unlatched the silver band that bound my hair. I shook my hair a little and ducked out of the kitchen.

"Aruna Firewife," the chief said. Beyond him a man slumped in the corner. The rider. He drank water, and his face was flushed pink from his cheekbones to his ears. The chief sighed, waiting.

"Backwa, Chechma Chief," the formality hurried out of me, and I waved my hand as if to hurry them more. It hadn't seemed the time for ceremony.

I sat in the chair Shen offered, and then the chief sat, too. A serving man brought carved wooden bowls of coffee, stained dark brown from years of use.

"The Rathodians are camped a day's ride from here," Backwa said. His body was old, but hard from a life of work. He looked hardly older than Shen, but darker and less happy. I expected then that I would look the same in a few years, as if I were made out of only bone and sand, instead of flesh and blood. Looking at the chief was like looking at a tree.

"Dinner sits a collection of gourds on the table," I had said to him, bold as can be. Light flickered in his eye, but he didn't move.

"They have finally come to fold us into Rathodia. We are to become Rathodians." He looked at me, a question in his eye, as if I were a stupid child.

"Of course I know what that means," I nearly shouted. Shen shuffled his feet beside me. Why did he still stand there like a man servant? I took a deep breath to cleanse the anger that was growing within my chest like the putrid heart sickness. I knew even then that the anger was fed by fear. Fear of losing the only way I had ever known. The only reason for being.

"They sit on their women," the man in the corner called to us, his voice cracking. The chief looked at him as if he were the son of a beggar sitting at his high table. Backwa looked as though he might spit, but he did not. Instead he said, "We need to decide if we are going to fight, or go peacefully."

"Are we prepared for such a fight? How many warriors have they? And we?"

"You have until sunup to give me your answer." I had been dismissed.

Back out in the air, I started walking, but not back toward the cook house. I walked toward the tree line with the hope that in among the trees no one would find me for a time and I could think. Word would have already gotten to the women's quarters about the decision to be made. When that happened in the past for small matters, like who should marry whom or what crops they should plant the coming planting season, I had been overwhelmed by the tribe's people who wished to sway my vote in one direction or another. I had been convinced of how well beets kept and how they worked wonders for the blood, and how we should plant parsnips instead of beets because they didn't stain our clothes or how we should plant beets because we could use them to stain our clothes beautiful shades of red. It had been maddening. But this decision required a clear head and hours of my most important thought. My decision would change the course of my people forever, and probably kill most of them besides. Shen still walked at my elbow. I had waited for him to drop off on his way elsewhere, but he didn't .

Stopping midstride, I turned to face him. I waited. I was not a woman known for my ability to hold my tongue once it began a journey.

"We probably aren't. They seem to have about thirty warriors, while we have twelve," he answered. "They could also send reinforcements if we manage to hold on for any length of time. We have the hills as the advantage. Higher ground is always good in a fight."

"Be careful when you use the word always," I had whispered. "They may just find a way to use it to their advantage."

"But we also have you." He smiled when he said it, as if he really believed that I were enough to make up the difference of 18 trained warriors wielding spears and arrows. I had smiled back at his confidence. His admiration. I had dared not hope that it was more.

"What is out here?" Shen asked. He motioned with his head in the direction we were going and had to squint into the blazing rays of the setting sun.

"My husband," I laughed, bitterness scaring the edges of the sound. He stopped and watched me walk ahead of him for a few spans. I reached the tree line before him and began gathering kindling. He jogged to catch up. He gathered with me, and we worked silently until a small fire was laid out in the ceremonial rock ring I privately used.

"You've been a friend to me these last three years. Shen." I had said his name quietly and slowly, as if it tasted like honey on my tongue.

"You talk as though you've made your decision."

"Fire is consumption. The tongues of the fire lick until there is no more fuel, and then they travel outward, searching for more. Fire gives us warmth and hot food and light, but it also takes away like a thief come under the blanket of night."

"Could you love me?" He asked the question straightforward and naïve. I studied his face for jest and found none. "Even a little, enough, so that we could be together, under Rathodian law?"

"Shen." His name felt like magic. I wanted it to be. I said it again. He mistook my meaning, was untouched by the magic, and he turned away.

"Please forgive me, Aruna Firewife." He smiled bitterly, laughing at himself. I told him he misunderstood me and the Rathodians.

"They will know who I am, Shen. They will take me. They will use me. They will kill me."

"I won't let them. I will hide you. Tell them you are my wife." He took my shoulders in his hands, touching me as I had not been touched since I was a child. He moved his desperate hand to my face. "You would have me, wouldn't you?"

I could not answer. The sound of the Rathodian warriors cresting the hills came to us on the wind. I was too late. Shen drew his sword and ran back toward his father's tents. He would die defending me, I had thought. For nothing.

The Rathodians came for me not long after I watched Shen's back disappear in the distance. I had wanted to run after him, stop him from going, run the other way. But a strength of honor held me like roots of a tree in the spot where I stood. The smoke from the fire drew them. They thought they were finding warriors or perhaps tribespeople caught unaware. They thought what they found would go easily. They wanted us, I knew, not for us but for our hands. We would work in their fields and in their mines and in their whore houses. If they didn't kill us, they would use us.

But I was a fire wife. I wouldn't come easily. Raising my hands out in front of me, I began chanting. The fire hissed its words to me, and I gave them voice, changing the air in the palms of my hands into fire. My skin stung as I sent the burning fire on the wind to the approaching warriors. They gasped and bent, drawing fire into their lungs. Some fell. They beat at the flames with their swords, but you can't fell magic like you do a man. I took the very fire into me and spread it across the wall of warriors with a wave of my arms. Their faces were red and then black. We are the people of the fire.

But more came, and the wall of warriors did not fall. The fuel of my fire dwindled, and soon it grew difficult to hold onto the flames. The place of change between fire and not fire grew wider. And then the Rathodian fire wife rode up on a horse the color of a cold day.

She slid off the horse, and I chanted again, my voice crackling like one of my fires. She was shorter then I, and older. Did I know her? She wore the red scars of many blisters, but I do not burn. I hated myself for wanting to give her more blisters.

"Is there no chance for talk?" I shouted over the rush of wind and flame. Her smile spoke of pity. She began to chant in a language I did not understand. It was not the language of the fire. I pushed against her, but my fire was too small and growing smaller until the last brand snuffed to smoke.

"What have you done?" I asked the crone as two Rathodians took my arms.

"What I am made to do," she answered.

I had not exaggerated when I told Shen that the Rathodians would take me and use me. What I didn't know, is that they would not favor me with death. Instead, their blade master used his sharpest knife and took my tongue.

A mind protects itself. My mind wrapped around me and forgot to think for days. When I woke up, the pain threatened to take back my consciousness and return me to the darkness of unknowing. Every swallow reminded me of how I wanted to die and how lucky I was to still be living. They had used my own friend fire to stop the blood. I reached out to the fire beside me with my mind. All my spells swirled in my head, but I could not utter the words. My magic was dead. When I was awake enough, they led me to the Odds Camp, where I was set free within the walls. The first few days it rained, and I stayed in the shelter with the old and the sick. Then I met Feather Woman.

I am always hungry.

***

Feather Woman and I stopped going to see the new arrivals. There weren't many now, and we had other concerns. Summer had arrived, and we stayed out of the sun when we could. I spent days staring at my upturned hands, listening to the fire speak, and waiting for the flame to appear. Once I thought I felt my palm tingle, but I was mistaken.

We collected rocks and made a better fire pit. We collected more rocks and made a picture with them in the dirt around our pit. We placed the rocks end to end in large spirals. They swept us away to another place, a place where we could see the stars and lie in the cool arms of the sea.

And then one day, he walked in through the gates, the last refugee. I saw him from our fire. The bowl of gruel slipped from my fingers when I saw him walk like a ghost through the camp. I half stood. Feather Woman looked from me to Shen and then back to me. She understood through all the pain that clouded her everyday thoughts that this man was who we had been waiting for all those days. She clapped her hands and repeated the sound "ya" over and over. I wanted to make her stop. I didn't want to share this moment with anyone but him. I pushed her out of my way and walked slowly to meet him.

His clothes hung on the angles of him. He shuffled his feet in the dirt and kept his hands outstretched in front of him as if he were feeling an invisible power welling up from the ground. And two black pits were burnt into the place where his eyes had been.

I made my first sound. A gargled cry left my throat without my bidding. I hadn't intended letting him know I was there. Death would have been kinder. But he heard and turned his face to me.

"Who's there?" he asked. The only sound I could make was three grunts to symbolize the three syllables of the name by which he knew me. I had not heard the name in months. I had thought there was no person living who knew me by that name. Shen shook his head. He didn't understand. I went to him. I took his hand, and I led it to my hair. Please remember, I thought at him. His hand cupped my head as if it had lain there a thousand times before. Oh, would that we had.

He leaned in close and touched his nose to my hair. I knew I smelled of sweat and blood and dung, but I also smelled of smoke. There had always been the smell of smoke about me. He lingered there, his nose in my hair, and then whispered, "Aruna?" I nodded my head to that he could feel it. Had he eyes, perhaps he would have cried. I did, but not for happiness. I took his hand again, and this time I put his fingers in my empty mouth.

He sobbed then, and I cried the tears that he couldn't. We were broken, and there was no peace that could heal us.

THANK YOU TO OUR SUPPORTERS

Many thanks to our patrons and supporters, especially:

**Stephanie Johnston • Cathrin Hagey
S Naomi Scott • Natalie Weizenbaum
Siobhan Beeman**

**Emily Anderson • Felicia OSullivan • J'nae Spano
Katherine Montalto • Kennon Hulett
Martin Cohen • Salomao Becker
Shannon White • Tamara Rutledge • Tory Hoke
Bonnie Warford • Kara • Frederick Stark**

**Brit Hvide • Carly Racklin • Charlotte Nash-Stewart
Dirck de Lint • GriffinFire • Isabel Cañas
Jocelyn Actual • Karen Anderson
Jen G • Kayla • Liz Warner
Maria Haskins • Suzanne Thackston**

Want to see your name here? Become a patron!
patreon.com/lunastation

About the Cover Artist

Corrine is an award-winning illustrator and designer working out of the Boston Area.

You can find more of her work at:

corinnereid.com

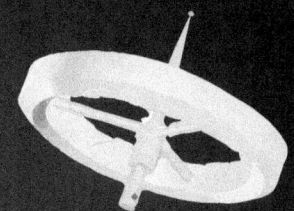

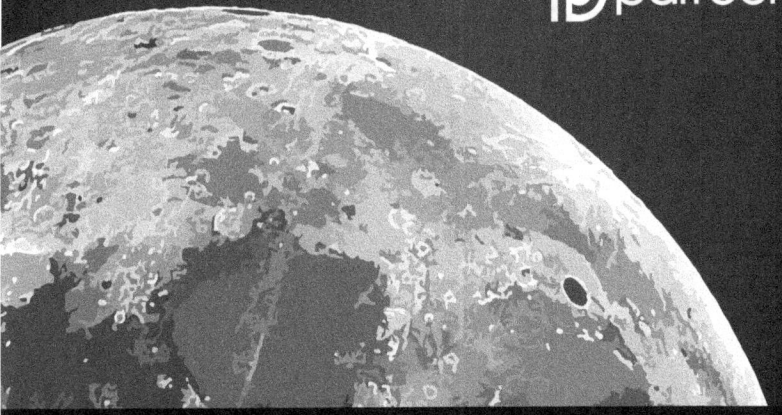

www.ingramcontent.com/pod-product-compliance
Lightning Source LLC
Chambersburg PA
CBHW070557130626
46556CB00001B/190